TREASON'S CROWN

ANNE WHEELER

ISBN: 978-1-951910-06-8 [print]
ISBN: 978-1-951910-05-1 [ebook]

For Meghan.

Kingdom of Nantoise
Mencote Desert
Tourmel Mountains
Kingdom of Meirdre
Kalcine River
Brannitz
Illrus River
Kingdom of Vassian

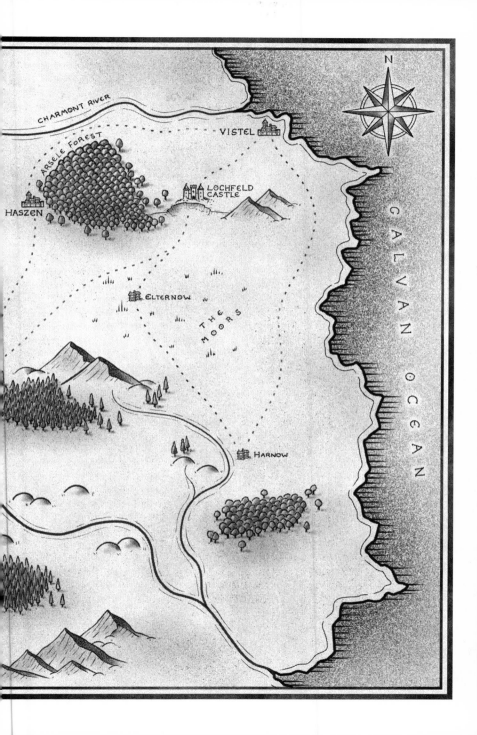

CHAPTER ONE

THE LAST OF THE FIREPLACE EMBERS WINKED OUT AS I pulled my shawl around my shoulders. The day had sped by, and I wasn't unhappy for the prospect of the relative warmth of my bed, for even the single candle next to me could scarcely keep burning in the draft leaking through the crack in the room's sole window. It had been there for two years, ever since the incident with the deer, and Papa couldn't afford to repair it, just like we couldn't afford to repair most things. The draft made winter evenings even more miserable than usual, but Mama insisted I complete my needlepoint before bed, and I had never been one to argue. I also wasn't given to ingratitude, not usually. At least we had glass, I continually reminded myself—some in our hamlet of

Elternow had resorted to oiled animal skins across gaping holes in their walls.

I'd done enough spring flowers for one winter night. I licked my chapped lips, then set the thread and hoop in the basket next to my feet and rubbed my sore neck before shivering again. The wind was not the only evidence of the storm the neighbors had predicted yesterday; wet snow was beginning to hit the window. Papa would struggle to reach the barn and feed the horse and cow in the morning, especially with the inflammation which had turned his fingers and knees into knotted messes. I was not allowed to help him any longer, and selfish though it might be, I was grateful for Mama's recent insistence on more feminine pursuits. Needlepoint and baking were tedious, to be sure, and her marital plans for me frightening, but at least they didn't involve trudging through snow.

I glanced at the candle, burnt to the bottom, but before I could blow it out, there was a knock on the door of our low stone house. A pounding, really. I called for Mama even before springing to my feet. A visitor in this weather, this time of night . . . Something was wrong. It was always that way. A poorly positioned calf, fire consuming a thatched roof, or even an intractable fever. Terrible things happened at night.

It had been night when they'd taken Thomas, after

all—a warm and breezy late autumn midnight, not like this wintertime evening—but night all the same. We'd heard the horses, which wasn't so unusual by itself, even in a poor village. But these had been more than a few lost travelers looking for shelter in the wildness of the moor. We'd huddled in this very room, Mama and Papa and me, knowing King Laurent had sent his men for a reason. And in the morning, when Elternow was down three men including Thomas, we learned what that reason was.

Would it be the same tonight?

I threw open the door, bracing myself against the cold, praying it wasn't something that required me and my nascent medical skills. My down blanket was calling me louder and louder by the moment, but more importantly, Mama would be furious if I left tonight to help. Every healer and midwife in Elternow was a woman, but that wasn't good enough for her. It wasn't *feminine enough*.

But this time, outside our house, fifty paces from the village proper, it wasn't a worried father who stood there, or even a villager covered in soot.

It was six of the king's men, snow swirling about them.

They weren't as flashy as in the paintings I'd seen in school, but I suspect that was due to the weather.

Heavy wool cloaks, lined with fur, covered their brocade tunics. I could imagine them anyway: royal blue silk, with a sheen unheard of in the fabric we spun here, laced with gold embroidery finer than I was capable of. I was stuck between fear and interest until my gaze landed on their swords.

My throat closed up at the sight of the polished steel. Mama and Papa had done no wrong, even though doing no wrong was harder and harder these days. The taxes were always paid on time, difficult as that order was, and they never spoke a word against the king.

None of us did. None of us associated with those who did.

Well.

Most of us didn't.

I stood there silently, my failure darting about in my mind, and one of the men, about the same age as my twenty summers, looked worriedly at the one with gold cord on the shoulders of his cloak.

"Do you think she's mute, Captain?" he asked. "He won't be happy."

I don't know what I expected. I held my breath, my eyes wide, just standing there in the doorway.

The captain burst into laughter. "I doubt she's

mute." His amusement faded. "But if she leaves us standing here in the cold, I may cut out her tongue."

My imperiled tongue darted to my lips once more, and somehow, I found the courage to speak. "You honor us with your presence, Captain. Please, do come in and warm yourselves." After what had happened to Thomas, I was nothing if not specific with the correct responses—when they finally came.

He nodded with the lightest of smiles, and six sets of boots tromped in behind me as I lay a forbidden extra log into the now-cooling fireplace. The coals caught at once, and I couldn't help but think that if a visit from our enemies was what it took to find extra warmth, maybe it was worth it.

"Riette!" My mother's shock was palpable behind me. I spun around to see her clutching a spare piece of fabric around her, her lips moving in a silent prayer. "What is this? What have you done?"

The captain interrupted before I could reply.

"Your daughter is showing us the hospitality the king requires of you. I urge you to do the same, Madame . . ."

"Kaleveld." Mama's hands fluttered as she pushed by me and set another log on the fire, more, I suspected, to distract attention from her mistake than to warm the room. The space had already grown sweltering with the eight of us. "And of course, Captain," she went on. "Anything you need."

"I need to speak with Master Kaleveld." The captain cleared his throat. "All of you."

"I'm here." Papa's voice was even as he entered, though wary. "It's ghastly weather for a ride from Lochfeld Castle, sir."

I brushed sweat from my forehead as the room closed in around me. If only I could wipe it from under my arms as well. Thomas was there, in the king's dungeons. We'd been seen together by neighbors and strangers alike before the royal guard bore down upon Elternow to arrest him for treason. Could these men be here—

"It was urgent," the leader said. "Even through a snowstorm. Next week is the Feast of St. Margaretha, you know."

"I am aware." Papa's wariness increased at the non sequitur.

"King Laurent needs a wife by then."

"A wife?" Something cold slunk down my spine.

"It is—" The captain looked at me, as if down his nose. "Difficult to explain. A tradition, if you will."

The explanation wasn't mocking, exactly, but confused me, nonetheless. The feast, yes, we all knew of that. But poverty muted that ancient celebration these days, and it was doubtful anyone in Elternow planned on celebrating at all—the pardon of criminals was an all but assured aspect of the festivities, although Thomas would never be absolved of his crimes.

"And you're coming for her?"

Mama had asked exactly what I was thinking. King Laurent's father had married a common woman, but that had been years ago, and it wasn't exactly something discussed on a routine basis. Perhaps it was some odd family preference.

Perhaps we were simply easier to control than noblewomen.

"It is not for me to question the king. Nor any of us. He will explain further if he deems appropriate." The captain looked around, his gaze landing on me. "But this is not a foregone agreement. You may say no."

Mama gasped. "And if she does?"

He held out his hand. A gold coin sat there, and I looked away in pain as the fire caught the edge, flashing like the light of sun directly into my eyes.

"If Miss Riette refuses, nothing will happen. We'll move on to the next house down the road. But if she says yes—this coin, plus more." His gaze fell on the window. "No broken glass. No rationing firewood. No gruel for dinner. Medicine for your husband, Madame

Kaleveld. You'll be taken care of for the rest of your lives."

"Which is how long?" I broke in. "A week?"

He raised his eyebrows, half in amusement, half in exasperation. "You read too many novels, Miss Riette. As long as your parents are loyal to the crown, they will stay alive, just like before. This is no trick."

I didn't bother to tell him that all our books had long since been burned for fuel, including the one with the paintings of the royal guard. "I suppose when you have a million times what your subjects have, it wouldn't be."

"Riette!"

If Mama didn't stop saying my name like that, I was going to scream.

"Please forgive my rudeness, Captain." Thomas's face popped into my mind, and suddenly, harassing them didn't seem wise any longer. My heart ached at the memory of his lips on my cheek. "I'm simply over-whelmed."

"Best become un-overwhelmed, then. I need your answer now. It's a long ride back, and I don't want to delay."

"Now?" My teeth chattered in contrast to the grow-ing, uncomfortable warmth.

"You may discuss with your parents first, if you must."

As if that were possible with half the royal guard standing in the same room. I looked at Mama and Papa, unsure of what to do. They stared in return, as if they weren't sure what to say, either—like they hadn't imagined this situation in a thousand years of dreaming.

"He said medicine." Tears formed as I made my decision, then I shrugged. "I can't say no."

"You needn't worry about that." Papa clasped his hands behind his back so I couldn't focus on his knuckles. How much longer would he be able to milk with those fingers? "I want this to be your decision. If one has to be made, you make it alone. Not me, not your mother."

"I'll go." I prayed he wouldn't ask me to explain the decision, because I didn't want to explain it to myself. "I don't see any other way. And it'll be all right."

Mama kissed my cheeks, tears streaming down her face. She didn't say anything, and her emotions irritated me. She had what she wanted for me—a husband, one better than I could ever find in Elternow. What was there to be this upset about it? King Laurent was horrid to our people, yes, and I didn't suffer any delusions that my future as his wife would be joyful, but my decision would benefit all of us in various ways. Why couldn't she see that?

"It's settled then." Papa grabbed me by the shoulders, like his hold would stop me from leaving. "What does she need to bring?"

One of the men, silent until now, chuckled. "I daresay she owns nothing worth bringing."

I ignored him and scooped up my embroidery basket. The once-hated pastime had become a lifeline to my entire world. "This. I'm bringing this."

The captain nodded. "I'm sure he'll allow it."

He swung the front door open again and gestured outside before I could grab my cloak. The heavy fabric around my shoulders, I swallowed, clutched the basket to my chest, and told myself that the chill which ran down my spine had everything to do with the way winter reentered the cottage—not with his words.

CHAPTER TWO

LOCHFELD CASTLE LOOMED HIGH ABOVE US, AND I settled back in my saddle to gaze up at the craggy cliffs upon which it sat. My bottom had become numb the day before, and the rest of me wasn't in much better shape, even though the snow had stopped, leaving the darkness streaked with the stars. The horse Captain Willem had set me on when we'd left Elternow was well-trained, and she trotted beside the group with little input from my frozen hands. A warhorse, certainly, but it seemed tonight we both wanted the same thing—a bed and warmth.

Willem gave another order, and we headed up a narrow trail in the rocks. I clung to the horse with all the strength I had left—I'd never been a particularly strong horsewoman—but my mare was steadier than I imagined. Hooves clopped as we climbed, scattering what rocks remained after the first half of winter. The wind was my enemy now, and on the unprotected hill side, it bit, fierce and raw, into my bare cheeks. I couldn't help but imagine what the king would say if he saw me looking like this. He'd not find me attractive, surely, and for some reason I found myself wishing he would.

Soon enough we reached the top, and from closer up, the castle didn't appear as foreboding as it had from below. Spires rose from the towers, sheer decoration rather than functional battlements. Candles flickered in most of the towering windows, and a few chambers were lit more brightly.

Fireplaces. In the past few days of riding and small fires at night, I'd almost forgotten what they looked like.

Willem eased his gelding over to me. "You'll not see him tonight. We'll need to get you thawed out and cleaned up, and if I'm not mistaken, you could use some sleep."

I concealed my panic at his use of *we* as we trotted across a stone bridge I could barely see through my fatigue and sudden anxiety. Surely this group of men wasn't going to take care of my toiletry needs. It'd been bad enough spending the past two nights alone in a tent while they camped nearby.

I needn't have worried, because when we galloped through the gate and into a small courtyard, a servant waited—a woman—fur around her shoulders. I slid from the saddle, limp, and she fixed Willem with a glare I'd have never been brave enough to attempt.

"Captain!" The woman wrapped her arm around me, and I practically fell into her warm embrace. "You shouldn't have ridden the child through that weather."

"It wasn't as though we could stay out there in that." Willem slid from his horse and shrugged. "She's used to it, anyway."

"I doubt that." The woman pushed me away to look me up and down. "She's not very sturdy."

"She made it this far, didn't she?" Willem grunted. "He'll make do."

Sturdy? That's what she expected? That's what the king expected? Of course I wasn't sturdy. We've been starved for the past twenty years.

The servant made a noise of dissent and motioned me into an alcove, then up a set of stairs. "It seems we have work to do. Let's get to it, then."

"It was a long ride, ma'am." Her rudeness regarding my disheveled appearance wasn't the last thing I expected, but it wasn't the first. I hated explaining myself, and the reason for my disheveled appearance should have been obvious, but perhaps it wasn't. Perhaps she'd never ridden two days through a snowstorm.

She eyed me sideways. "None of that ma'am nonsense. I'm Sara."

"Sara." I tested the name. It was so normal. "You've been in the castle long?"

"I was born here." We turned down a corridor lit with oil lamps, and I tried to ignore the muddy tracks I left behind us. "During the first King Laurent's reign."

"I see. You served his wife?"

"Until her death, yes." Her eyes brightened a bit. "It will be nice to have a queen around the castle again. It's a different feel, a better environment. Loneliness doesn't become a king, after all, and Lochfeld has been too empty of late."

For some reason, the word *queen* unnerved me, like I hadn't made the connection between it and my upcoming marriage until now. I fell silent as I followed Sara down empty corridor after corridor until we arrived at what I assumed would be my new home. She threw open the door, and my mouth fell open at the sight which greeted me.

Not one but two fireplaces burned inside. A silk rug the size of our living room back home lay before one, and a wooden tub full of steaming water sat in front of the other. I drew my stare from the water long enough to take in the canopy bed and matching silk chair beside it. Both were a shade of red rarely seen in Elternow. Dye that vibrant was too expensive to use for anything except selling to noblewomen passing through our town on their way to something better. I must have looked like a fool staring as I was, but I couldn't take my eyes off it.

Sara clapped her hands, and with a shock, I realized there were two other servants in the room, their heads close together as they giggled. Hoping they would blame the flush on my cheeks on the fire, I looked down at my sodden shoes.

"Get her in the tub," Sara ordered. "There isn't much time until sunup, and she needs some rest before then."

Feeling the order was meant for me as much as the servants, I stripped off my muddy dress. Sara clucked her tongue, likely at how my ribs were much more prominent than any woman would prefer, then poured a glass of wine from the decanter on a nearby table. I ignored her unspoken commentary and sank into the water.

Bliss.

She shoved the glass into my hand. "Drink this. Soak for a while, then we'll get you cleaned up."

It was a simple enough order. I obeyed, though the

wine was stronger than anything I'd ever tasted. Papa kept malt in the barn for medicinal purposes, but he'd always forbidden me from drinking it myself, though I suspected he partook some nights. If it tasted anything like this, I couldn't blame him. The spice rolled around my tongue, and my eyes grew heavier. Soon, they closed completely, and I basked in the certain knowledge my attendants would never let me drown. Maybe being taken care of wouldn't be so awful after all. I was seconds away from falling asleep when a shout echoed outside.

"Sara—he wants her now!"

It was Willem, and he sounded panicked. I jerked upright, alarm likely written all over my face. The way the two younger servants were flailing about only added to the commotion, but Sara clapped her hands again and began to issue orders. I was pulled from the tub, hair damp but without soap, then forced into stays much lovelier than the ones I'd left at home. One of the girls pinned up my hair in a rather haphazard fashion to keep it off whatever dress they planned to shove me into, and my breath became short.

I'd hoped to have more than an hour to adjust to my new situation, and it seemed as though Sara had expected the same. But they drew a heavy velvet gown over my head, and I realized this was for real. The king had summoned me in the middle of the night—of course someone had informed him I'd arrived—and I was to meet him, frightened and exhausted and wet as I was. I shook with that understanding as one of the girls pinned my hair up, Sara giving her suggestions the entire time.

"It's still damp," she said, biting her lip so hard it turned white, "and we'll need to have your things fitted better tomorrow, but I suppose there's nothing to be done about that now. He'll be understanding. There was only so much we could do to prepare."

"Sara—" I hesitated before I asked the stupid question. "What am I—how am I supposed to act?"

She stared at me, her lips still pressed together in frustration.

"Two days ago, I'd had no thoughts of ever meeting any king," I added. "I don't want to make a mistake."

She grabbed me by the shoulder and ushered me out into the silent corridor. "Stay silent. Curtsy before him. Low. He'll tell you when to stand. Answer his questions and say nothing else until you're dismissed. And for heaven's sake, try not to stare like an awed peasant."

She rattled off more rules as we raced down the stairs. I tried to listen, but between my growing headache and trying not to stumble in my new shoes, it was a losing battle. By the time we arrived at the iron door of the throne room, I was out of breath and half asleep.

The two guards on either side of the doorway wore the gleaming uniforms I'd imagined the night the soldiers had arrived on my doorstep. They opened the door as we approached, and though Sara took a step back, I peered inside. The space was smaller than I believed a throne room should be, but if the silk in my bedroom had been a surprise, the deep blue fabric covering every bit of the walls made my heart race. A carved chair sat at the end, though I couldn't identify any of the designs from this distance, and on it—

On it sat a man.

CHAPTER THREE

I COULDN'T SEE MUCH OF HIM FROM THE DOORWAY—IN fact, his indigo tunic all but blended into the silk walls —but his body language gave him away. He was impatient. That was clear from the way he'd placed a hand no-so-casually on the arm of the throne when the door had opened, and I froze, without regard for his upcoming annoyance.

"You'll go in alone," Sara whispered in my ear, drawing back. "This is not a place for me. Go!"

Fine. If I could survive everything I had so far in life, I could survive this. Resisting the urge to pick up my long skirts, I walked inside, my head high. I might not own much of anything any longer, but I had my pride.

The throne was farther away than it'd appeared at

first, and I kept my eyes on it as I went. Analyzing my situation with a detached appreciation was easier than actually experiencing it. In the corners of my eyes, oil burned within glass sconces—the sheer number lit seemed odd for the middle of the night, but I knew their purpose at once. He wanted to see me, and not in the dim of an unlit throne room. A figure stood next to him—he didn't want to be alone with me. Something sparkled on the throne—had he dressed up for this introduction just like I had?

Sara's warnings flickered into my head, and I came to a stop at what appeared to be an appropriate position, then held a low curtsy. I doubted Papa would have approved of the action, but then, he'd have done the same regardless of his feelings, wouldn't he? Thomas wouldn't have, and that's why he was locked up in a cell somewhere.

A tear ran down my cheek at his memory, and I lowered my head further.

"Riette."

Fabric rustled; wood creaked. King Laurent was standing. My heart pounded so hard he must have been able to see it, but I took a breath and remained still.

"Straighten." His voice was colder than when he'd said my name. "Let me see you."

I did so, praying he didn't notice the tear. He

circled around me, and as his shadow drifted to my side, I chanced a look up. The figure next to the throne was Willem, and he jerked his chin downward, so I did the same. An insolent order it was, but I would take whatever help I could get.

"Your hair is wet," the king went on.

From so close, I could study his clothing—from the knees down, at least. His boots were worn, which I found strange. Perhaps he enjoyed riding. His breeches were of the finest leather, though, and it was impossible to keep my eyes down instead of appreciating whatever luxurious fabrics made up the rest of his clothes. Realizing I'd been staring even if from under my eyelashes, I swore in my mind, words I'd picked up from listening to Thomas's men.

"I am sorry, sire. We didn't realize—"

"Silence! There will be no excuses. The next time you enter this room, you will be presentable."

Heavens. How long would I suffer this embarrassment? Fifty years? More?

"Yes, sire," I replied, making a mental note only to wash my hair when he was away from the castle. What else could I say? Anything else would be an excuse, though I desperately wanted to tell him the other option would have been for me to have appeared before him covered in mud.

"Good." His shadow retreated a few paces, then he stopped. "Come. Sit."

Willem pulled a plain wooden chair up beside the throne as I approached, and I was acutely aware of the intentional contrast between it and the ornate chair on which he sat. I adjusted my skirts and took a seat, keeping my eyes lowered.

"So. This is Riette Kaleveld. She is rather lovely, don't you agree?"

Willem made a non-committal noise, and I cringed at the idea of them talking about me like I wasn't there.

"Though I should have known her hair would be brown. They always are from Elternow."

The comment wasn't directed at me. Further, it sounded like he knew me—knew *of* me, that was—and tendrils of fear curled about my spine. Or was it just the bones of my stays?

"Yes, sire, it seems they are." Willem, to his credit, agreed without a wisp of irony.

"And her eyes are blue."

"They are."

"You know of my preferences. She is not it."

"It was the first house. She was the first one to agree. You know the law, sire."

In the corner of my vision Willem shrugged, and I envied his indifferent tone. Would I ever be able to effect such a manner in the king's presence? I doubted it.

"Yes. I know it." King Laurent sighed. "She'll have to do, then."

"*I'll* have to do?" It took a moment before I realized the words were mine. "You don't need to treat me like I'm your last choice!"

His eyebrows flew up, and I focused again on the marble floor, waiting for a slap on the cheek—or worse. Instead, I heard laughter.

"Perhaps you would be, if things were different. But the law is specific, and here you are." I must have looked confused, even staring at the floor, so he went on. "You don't know why you're here, do you? It's very simple. I'm not growing any younger, and I have no wife, no heirs. A king without either is a liability to his own self. Weak-appearing. Someone his rivals can jump on. My advisors have convinced me of this truth, and what better time for a wedding than the Feast of St. Margaretha?"

He cleared his throat. "As for my choice of a bride, my line has selected from common women for the past five generations. The pool of noblewomen is shrinking by the decade, and if we wish to continue with strong heirs—well, your father is a farmer. You can figure it out—or ask one of the servant women later if you must."

I had assumed it was something like that, but hearing it explained so bluntly, especially in front of two men, made me blush anew. There had never been any question that I was to become the neighbor's stallion, borrowed to inject new life into an old bloodline, but—but his candor was intolerable. I hated to destroy my parents' dreams of a better future, but I couldn't subject myself to this humiliation, even for pretty dresses and medicine.

"I'm sorry sire, but—is this agreement permanent?" The question flew out before I could stop myself. I wanted to flee, but I'd do it safely.

"Do you take me for a monster?" He lounged back on the throne as I swallowed, hard. "No. Not until the ceremony. I'd be disappointed, naturally, but I realize this life isn't for everyone, so until then, you're free to leave."

My shoulders relaxed.

"But I doubt Willem told you all of what you'll gain after the wedding. You may have been the lucky first, but you don't know all of what I'm offering."

"He showed us the coin." The image of it laying in Mama's palm made me second-guess my decision to flee. Why must these decisions be so difficult? "We are grateful for it."

But we wouldn't need it if you didn't treat us so poorly.

"And the extra head of cattle and medicine for your father, yes. But I think I can offer you something you'll appreciate more than money and pretty dresses."

I looked at him then, and really saw him for the first time. He might have had ten years on me, but no lines showed in his face—the product of better food, more sleep, and less work than anyone in Elternow would ever experience. His hair was shorter than most wore it these days, and I couldn't understand his issue with my eyes, since his were just as blue. He wasn't unattractive in the least, especially with the thick lashes that framed his eyes, and I could have stared at him for hours had he been anyone else. Instead, I found a crack on the floor and spoke again.

"What else can you offer me?"

"Something I think you'll find very difficult to turn down." He chuckled. "On the eve of every royal marriage, the bride chooses a prisoner to free."

"The—the bride?" My answer was uneven.

"You know where the tradition of clemency during the Feast of St. Margaretha originates, do you not?"

"I do not, sire. I'm sorry."

He might have huffed at my ignorance had he been anyone else. Instead, his explanation came as tolerantly as a patient schoolmaster.

"Five hundred and seventeen years ago, the war between us and the Duchy of Conzell reached its fiercest point. Almost a stalemate. King Arend had captured the Duke of Conzell, but at what cost? The duke's army was stronger, and our people were starving —it was very likely Meirdre would come to ruin. So, they made a deal, in the very dungeon below this castle —a treaty, if you will. Arend would marry the duke's daughter, incorporating the duchy into Meirdre. Hostilities would cease, our people would have food once more, and there would be peace."

"What did the duke get from that?" I asked. "It doesn't sound like a sensible proposal."

"His life, I suppose, even though he would have lived it out in a cell. He was a coward and gave up his lands—and a war his people could have won—to save himself. 'Twould have been better for him to die with honor."

I could understand the duke's desire to live. I hated having what the king surely would have believed to be dishonorable thoughts—rebellious ideas seemed too dangerous here in Lochfeld Castle—but I could understand it.

"On the eve of their wedding, the story goes, Arend asked his new bride why she looked so unhappy. It was a rather silly question, since her father was being held

hostage three stories below where she'd said her vows—
and through her tears, she told him so. Unfortunately,
there wasn't much the king could do. If he released her
father, he would appear weak, and fragility was the last
thing he needed to show in the wake of a war." He
smiled. "But his bride proposed a solution. She would
select a prisoner to be released as a wedding gift to her,
allowing both her father his freedom and her husband
to save face."

"That's rather romantic." It *was*, if you ignored the
whole dungeon and prisoner and death part of it.

"They made a tradition of it from then on, one
that's been passed down through the ages, eventually
conflating itself with the Feast of St. Margaretha. In
recent years my advisors have taken on the role of
selecting prisoners, but I usually have one or two names
who are, of course, added to the list. This year . . . well,
I have no problem showing that I can be capable of
mercy when it suits my need. And I must confess, I do
prefer the original—and as you say, *romantic*
—tradition."

He was speaking in circles. "I don't understand."

"For this celebration, I'm doing something different. The choice has been given to you. Like Queen
Katrien, I want this to be a wedding gift from me to
you. Choose a prisoner."

Choose a prisoner.

I gasped. The words floated between us, making my head spin. Had I really heard them? Perhaps escape was the wrong plan of action.

He took my hand, then continued evenly. "Anyone. Even a traitor from the hangman's noose."

CHAPTER FOUR

My shoes, I realized for the first time, were embroidered with stars, the quality far beyond my own capabilities. I tried to count the stitches as the king let his comment hover in the smoky air of the throne room, but they were so delicate I gave up and met his stare.

"Choosing a prisoner to liberate must be a difficult decision, sire," I said. "I can only hope I do our people justice in choosing."

His eyes sparked with amusement, like the stars on my shoes. "Is it so difficult, Riette?" he asked. "I've recently learned you have a favorite among that unfortunate group—but perhaps I was given poor information."

His confirmation should have been a warning, but

instead it emboldened me. His men had tortured Thomas, Thomas had given up my name. King Laurent was no longer simply the king, and I was no longer cowering—we were two equals on solid footing, negotiating with all the information. Chance and tradition had brought us together, and he wouldn't squander the opportunity.

"Thomas Wennink? He's hardly a favorite, though I won't deny I know him. I even believed I loved him once," I said. "But childlike love means nothing in the grand scheme of things."

Whatever King Laurent thought of that statement, it wasn't a betrayal of Thomas, not exactly. Our relationship had always been fleeting. I'd had stars in my eyes at the idea of the leader of Elternow's rebellion group paying attention to me, and he enjoyed the kisses he was able to steal when I led the cow to pasture. It gave me a particular status in the village and him some pleasure in a life that was otherwise uncertain.

Did I truly love Thomas? Maybe. Most of the time, I believed I did. But marriages were rarely based on love, or I wouldn't have agreed to Willem's invitation so easily.

Did I believe Thomas would be the one to help overthrow the throne and restore peace and prosperity to our kingdom? Yes. Most definitely.

The king looked at me with fresh interest. "I won't permit adultery. If you think this will enable you to take advantage of my generosity and be with him as well . . ."

Offended, I lifted my chin. "I uphold my oaths."

In truth I'd never spoke one, and I had the sudden realization that I had no intention of doing so in the future. There was no way the king would let Thomas go, no matter the tradition, even if I married him. I knew now that I was being lied to. But I was here in the castle now, a place I'd never gain access to otherwise, and I could do something about his imprisonment. I had always known I'd risk anything and everything to free him for the sake of the rebellion, and now I had my chance. I would free Thomas or die trying.

"I believe you—though I shouldn't. We have an agreement, then?"

I nodded, even though my heart hadn't stopped pounding. "We do. I marry you; you release him."

"It's settled, then. The feast is in five days, if you can be ready by then. Anything you need to prepare, the servants will help you with." His eyes sparkled with as much humor as I suspected he ever deigned to show. "Make sure your hair is dry for the ceremony."

Five days. My heart thumped against the stays. Thomas might be doomed, but he would be alive for at least another five days, and that gave me plenty of time to figure something out. Images flooded my mind as the hope began to build. Thomas and I, galloping down the trail cut into the cliff. Presenting him to his resistance group, now broken up and in hiding. Saying goodbye as they rode off to do whatever it was they did. Watching him drive a sword through the king's chest.

King Laurent stood, interrupting the vision, and I flinched, unsure of what to do with him hovering over me. "Willem, send her back to her room. Make certain she gets some sleep and for heaven's sake, ensure she dries her hair. She can't be seen around the castle looking like this."

"Of course, sire."

I curtsied quickly. Willem gestured toward the rear doors, and I didn't risk a look back as my shoes padded away on the hard stone, though I could feel the king's stare on my back. Did he suspect what I had planned? The castle appeared so deserted that I must have a chance, but then again . . .

My hope flitted away like the smoke from the oil lamps above us. It was the middle of the night. Naturally the corridors of the castle were empty. There was no doubt the place would come alive soon—in the next five minutes, for all I knew—and my plan which had seemed effortless and certain in the throne room was already in danger. For now, I would also ignore the fact that saving Thomas would take away my parents' newfound financial prosperity and Papa's medicine.

Sara clucked at me when Willem left me in my room once more.

"Keeping you up half the night. Far be it from me to question him, but he should have known better," she said, tugging the heavy dress over my head. "The sun will be up soon, and then you'll need a tour and introductions, but first . . ." She frowned at my stays, then began to undo them. "One hour to rest, my lady. Then I'm afraid you'll have to begin your new life."

I muttered my thanks and slid into sheets that were quite possibly more expensive than the dress she'd yanked so unceremoniously off my body. As my eyes closed, I wanted, more than anything, to dream of home and the cracked glass in the living room window.

Instead, I dreamed of oubliettes and screams.

CHAPTER FIVE

It wasn't Sara who woke me, but a rooster somewhere far below my window. Morning was always a time of renewal, and today was no different, even in the castle of a man I hated. I whispered a quick prayer before slinging my feet to the floor and letting my toes dig into the rug. As the first knock came, I tried to tug the yards of fabric over my head, but only succeeded in tangling myself in velvet. When hands gently lifted it off me again, I froze.

"Apologies." The owner of the hands spoke. "But you didn't answer, and by the sound of fabric catching on goodness knows what, it seems you needed help."

"I—I'm Riette." The fabric cleared my head. She was my age, though more fashionably dressed than I'd ever been before yesterday, and her educated accent unnerved me. "And I'm not used to such a dress. I'd appreciate the help."

"So I see." She laughed and unceremoniously dumped the dress over my head, then arranged my skirts and tied the back with more skill than I possessed. "And I'm Juliana."

"Not a servant." Her gown, all velvet and silk, and the enormous emerald on her left hand belied her status. This was a courtier who would have sneered at me yesterday.

"Aren't we all servants to the crown?" Juliana laughed again, making me doubt my previous accusation. "I'm to keep you company. Show you around and make sure you're comfortable. Help you set up the rest of your household—that sort of thing."

"I appreciate that." She finished fastening the dress, and I turned to face her. "I'm to have my own household?" It was an overwhelming thought.

"You didn't expect the king to share your quarters, did you?" Juliana smiled, but there was no malice behind it. "This room is yours—he's not even allowed in. He's close by though, for—for after."

I reached for the glass of water that someone had filled while I was asleep. "Not allowed? I'm surprised anything is forbidden from him."

She waved an indifferent hand. "I suspect the ban is

of his own making. He's not interested in whatever goes on in women's lives. That part of the castle will fall to you."

"Perhaps you should show me around?" I suggested. "It was so dark and quiet when I arrived last night—I'm afraid I have no idea of where I am and where anything else is."

"Patience." She gave the door a sharp look, and as if on cue, it opened, admitting Sara, who carried a tray of fruit and bread. "Let her do your hair. You should have something to eat, then we'll be off."

Reluctantly, I sat before a large mirror, but I couldn't do much more than pick at a few dried strawberries while Sara arranged my hair on top of my head. It was the pins she used which were responsible for my distraction—the perfect tool for breaking into a dungeon. I answered her questions about the preference for my hairstyle and Juliana's innocent questions of my life before coming to the castle, but my soul was screaming for escape. No one would have understood my desire to flee if I'd spoken of it, and it took an entire five minutes to understand my motivation myself.

My own impatience was my biggest threat.

Finally, Sara released us, and I scampered down the stairs next to Juliana faster than I had when King Laurent had summoned me. More guards filled the corridors at this time of day, and they bowed at Juliana while giving me the briefest of nods. She was someone of importance based on how they treated her, but I didn't dare ask who or why.

"These are the stables." As we walked out an open doorway to one of the sizeable courtyards that made up the castle proper, Juliana waved at the long, tiled-roof building in front of us. "My Starduster is there, and if you're willing to ask the king for your own, we can go for a ride one day."

I hated telling her that I had no uses for horses except as a fast way to warn Thomas's men that the royal guard was coming. Spilling my secret at a resistance lookout seemed a good way to end up with a rope around my neck. Instead, I nodded.

"I would like that. Is there much time for such pursuits?"

"More than you had before, I would guess." Her forehead creased, and she ducked her head to the side before continuing. "I'm sorry. I'm afraid I'm going to step all over myself for the next few days. It's a fault of mine. I didn't mean—"

As we'd ridden up the cliffs last night, I'd decided I wanted to hate anyone who lived at Lochfeld. But Juliana's embarrassment was obvious and earnest. How could anyone hate her?

"I'm not offended," I replied. "I was hardly a laborer before, though I thought as much most of the time when Mama ordered me to do embroidery and read music and practice my language work." I laughed for the first time since arriving. Mama had done the best she could, expecting me to catch no more than a farmer with two horses, and here I was, about to marry a king.

"Oh! You can embroider?" Juliana's sweet face became, if it was possible, even more animated as she grabbed my arm. "We'll have to find you supplies for your needlework. You've never used silk, have you?"

"No, no, Juliana." Even though I'd brought my own thread, the horror of being forced into more embroidery practice before my escape was worse than almost anything else. Knowing she'd never understand that, I stumbled through an explanation. "I'm not good at it. Rather slow actually. Anyway, there's a piece I'd like to finish before I start anything else, and I'm afraid the silk would clash with what I've been using."

"Oh. Yes, of course." She pulled me along, and her smile brightened. "Perhaps after you finish, you can select something from my stock."

"That would be lovely," I managed to stammer. The idea of having someone to share my pain with wasn't wholly without charm, but I would be gone long before I finished the flowers on which I was already working.

We passed by the stables and into another wing of the castle, and I pulled her to a halt as a barred door passed off our left side. The corridor on the other side was lit with lamps even at this time of day, but it became dark toward the opposite end where only a single tread of a stairwell was visible. A cool breeze brushed my cheek when I walked by, and my intuition told me what was below.

"Juliana"—I tugged her to a halt at the door —"what is that?"

She blinked and tried to pull me forward, but I ground my feet into the stone.

"The stairwell to the dungeon, naturally," she said, tugging at my sleeve.

I held my breath. The first step of my plan would come sooner than I expected. "Could we visit?"

"Visit!"

"The king told me last night that I'd be selecting a prisoner to release on the eve of our wedding. In my mind, the best course of action would be to speak with the jailer and learn who is most deserving of that mercy."

Her rosy cheeks went pale, and she jerked forward,

away from the dungeon door. "That would be inappropriate."

"You're afraid."

"Hardly." Her footsteps grew heavier and her breath rapid as she led me out another door into yet another courtyard. I'd never learn my way around the castle at this rate. "Well, fine. I *am* a little afraid. Who wouldn't be?"

"Have you ever been down there?" Even a basic map of the underground prison would be useful.

"Once." She sighed and leaned against a stone wall, only to pick at a sad-looking pear tree that, sheltered under an overhang as it was, had somehow survived this late into the season. "King Laurent had gotten some notion into his head that prisoners would be allowed to celebrate Sommermas. I took a basket of spiced peaches down and gave them to the jailer. That was all. It was duty, and it was —it was horrible. It took the servants two weeks of trying to get the stench out of that dress. The king hasn't suggested such a thing since, and I haven't been back. I wish I could forget the things I heard and saw there."

She sounded traumatized, but she was a sheltered noblewoman. I'd been raised on a farm outside of a small village. I could handle it.

"Spiced peaches," I replied. "How odd."

"Probably poisoned. I didn't ask, and I'd rather forget." Juliana dropped the rose leaves to the ground and pointed out another wing. "That's the chapel over there—where you'll marry. Let's go see."

She was changing the subject, and I didn't want to think about someone poisoning Thomas under the guise of charity, so I followed her through a narrow alley and into the building. The single church in Elternow had glass—uncracked, we always made sure of that—but there wasn't any to be found in the walls here. Consistent with the castle's original use as a fortress, even a place meant to worship God was built like the rest of the castle, with thick stone walls and no entry points for arrows or enemies or bullets to enter.

The constant reminder of war and strife was depressing in a way, but I attempted to focus on the good. A chamber organ sat to one side, a stack of paper on top. I had no idea how to read music, but for the first time since I'd decided to rescue Thomas instead of marrying my sovereign, I wished I could stay and run my fingers over those keys until I could manage a song. For now, I'd enjoy the daydream and the sensation of something holier than myself.

I turned toward the altar, trying to decipher the saints portrayed on the icons surrounding. St. Margaretha at least should have been familiar, if not out of actual familiarity, then gratitude. She'd brought me here, after all—she would be responsible for Thomas's release. Squinting at the squares, each engraved in gold, I mouthed the ones I recognized.

"Riette." Juliana hissed my name, and when I turned from the altar, she was standing beside a side table that held—

I gasped, my eyes wide.

Two crowns.

One of them was large, heavy, studded with blue stones that I assumed were sapphires. Not that I'd ever seen such a thing, but the other girls talked about them sometimes. It was obviously King Laurent's, and I didn't give it much more thought than that.

Because the one that sat next to it took my breath away.

Lighter than the king's but hardly delicate, it was a subtler gold, rimmed with colored stones of all hues. From the azure of the sky, the emerald of the woodlands, and the rose and amethyst of the blossoms that dotted the moors around Elternow, it was the Kingdom of Meirdre turned a priceless work of art.

Soon to be *my* crown.

Juliana waggled her eyebrows in enthusiasm and pointed, but I shook my head. "I can't touch that!"

I backed away, more disturbed by her excitement

than anything else. It seemed to be some grave offense to try it on, especially since I had no plans of ever wearing it on my head for more than thirty seconds.

"Please," she insisted. "It's absolutely stunning, and I want to see it on you. And this wing is empty—no one will see!"

It was empty, like she said. Emptier than I thought it would be, which was strange. Shouldn't a castle be filled with advisors and courtiers and nobles? So far there'd only been a few servants, the king, and Juliana.

It didn't seem appropriate to ask about the state of the place, so I forced myself to smile before I crossed the marble to take a closer look. Juliana was right—the crown was stunning. At home, its gems would have been ostentatious, but here, they were understated.

"I do wish I could try it on." I glanced sideways at her. Grave offense or not, it was so tempting that I almost felt as though the crown was calling to me. And why wouldn't it? I'd never owned so much as a gold ring before.

"You should." Her smile grew broader. "After all, we'll have to see how it looks on you so we can figure out just the right way to style your hair. The fashions in the paintings aren't in style anymore, and Sara will need direction."

"You're so practical." A chuckle burst forth from my lungs.

"Always. Here, turn around."

I obeyed, with one last touch of my unadorned hair. Weight settled onto my head, and I laughed again.

"What's so funny?" Juliana sounded disapproving this time, and I wondered if I'd insulted her.

I couldn't have explained it to her, didn't know myself. "I'm not sure," I said. "I think I'm just thinking of the headache I'll have after wearing this for hours on my wedding day."

She made another noise of disapproval and came around in front of me. "It's enchanting," she replied, tucking some of my curls back while pulling others down. "Like it was made for you. I wish you could see it right now."

I glanced around, but there were no mirrors in the chapel, naturally. It was a place to focus on God, not on such silly things as looks, and while Juliana continued to express her admiration, I decided that was for the best. I'd stand here for an hour staring at myself if I could, and the weight was already bothering me—not to mention I was enjoying the approval and wealth more than someone of my status should. Than any woman should, really.

"Juliana—take it off, please." I rubbed the back of

my neck, the pain increasing by the second. "We'll have to find some other way to figure out how to do my hair, because this thing is hurting me already. It must be pulling on my hair or something."

"Strange." She did what I asked and placed the crown back on the table, then went back to fussing with my curls. "It's really very light."

"I'm not used to having anything on my head." Not something this uncomfortable, anyway. "I suppose I'll just need to get used to it."

At that, Juliana frowned in my direction. "Are you feeling all right? You've gone quite pale." Her hands began to wind in and out with each other. "Oh, no—I should have never been so selfish. I've overdone it, and you with hardly any sleep for the past three days. Let's get you back upstairs to lie down for a bit."

I wanted to snap at her that I felt fine, that I wasn't so weak that a few nights of poor sleep were going to do me in, but the truth was, I wasn't fine. The icons surrounding the altar had disappeared into a chaotic vision of wavy lines and sparkles, and looking at the white marble floor instead didn't do enough to steady my balance. If this was nothing more than a headache, it was proving to be an unusual and terrifying one. I'd have to ask Sara to find a surgeon who could procure some herbs for me, and on my first day no less, like some invalid. Surely the king wouldn't want a convalescent as a wife. Would he send me home before I had a chance to save Thomas?

Lost in those fears, I clung to Juliana's arm as she led me through the castle, my vision growing worse by the second. Fatigue? Dehydration? Stress? All of them and then some? Being able to identify the cause while being unable to treat myself would have been amusing if my sudden pain and the spots that floated through my field of vision weren't such a vexation. Nausea joined the undulating lines, and I focused so hard on not throwing up that I couldn't tell if she was retracing our steps or not.

Soon enough, the hard stone under my feet turned soft, but not rug soft. Wood? I blinked down at my feet, and to my surprise, my vision had cleared. The headache still raged somewhere in the background, but I was able to ignore it enough to bask in the return of my sight. Juliana came to a stop as I did, and I looked cautiously at her through my eyelashes, praying the awful sparkles wouldn't return.

"Where are we?" I asked. "This pattern—it's so random."

Juliana ran her fingers across my forehead and squinted down at the floor. "This is the grand ballroom. It's a map of Meirdre. See?" She skipped a few steps to my left, caution still written all over her face. "Here's Lochfeld Castle. The cliffs you rode up are here, and this"—she stepped back a few more paces—"is Elternow."

I massaged my temples as I looked around. When I stepped back and looked at the floor as a whole, it made sense. "That's why it seemed so random," I replied. "I was staring at the border with Kelsen."

Juliana pointed. "And Cardon is over here."

"This must have taken months to create." Of all the things I'd seen since arriving at the castle, besides the queen's crown, the map was the most impressive. Each boundary, each mountain range depiction, each village and outpost had been created by small insets of darker and lighter wood. Light oak ships floated through a sea of ebony to our east, and the forests were painstakingly arranged in a bark that shone a vague green. I paced along the border of Nantoise, to our north, my headache forgotten.

"It's exquisite, isn't it?" Juliana asked.

I nodded, fascinated, as I traced the path of the Charmont River that separated us from Nantoise with my foot. A small segment of the border north of the river sparkled in the light of the lamps above us, drawing me closer.

"What's so special about this section?" I asked, kneeling.

Juliana frowned from above. "Nothing that I'm aware of. Why?"

"The craftsman set this piece with diamonds." I'd never seen diamonds before an hour ago, but I suspected that's what they would look like in a floor. "Look, right here on the border by the sea. How odd."

"Diamonds?" She lowered herself to the floor next to me and ran her fingers over the glittering line. "Riette, this is mahogany."

"No, no, it's—it's lit, as if from within." It was too hard to explain what I was seeing, so I sat back on my heels and rubbed my head. "I'm seeing things again. I think my headache's coming back, and worse than before."

"Time for a rest then, and no argument." Juliana pulled me to my feet and eased me toward the door. "We don't have much time before the festivities begin, and we need you in perfect shape. The king will be furious if things are delayed because I've made you ill."

I looked back once as she dragged me from the ballroom.

The border was still glowing.

CHAPTER SIX

I HAD JUST POKED MY FINGER FOR THE THIRD TIME IN fifteen minutes when Sara came knocking on my door. More than happy to set the needlework aside, if only for a moment, I sprang from my chair, a smile on my face.

Juliana had forced me to bed immediately after reaching my room, and while I lay on my back with a cool rag over my head, she'd found two servants to keep me company and take in a few of my new gowns. It wasn't the way I'd wanted to meet my future helpers, but she wouldn't allow me back on my feet. Instead I'd closed my eyes and listened to them chatter about court intrigue while they tailored my clothing—intrigue which to their minds, appeared to involve which new courtiers were single and if said courtiers would *ever* make an appearance at Lochfeld.

My headache was gone by the time Juliana ushered them out, so she'd shoved me into a chair and placed my embroidery basket in my lap. I hadn't been certain staring at my hoop and fabric was any improvement over my headache, but I counted and knotted and cut thread with a diligence Mama would have been proud of.

"He wants to see you at once," Sara whispered, undoing my gown and yanking it off my head as she spoke. She hadn't glanced at the hem, yet she seemed to know how muddy it would be. Juliana and I hadn't been careful on our tour. "At least your hair will do tonight. We'll just get you into something clean and be off."

I didn't protest as she attired me in something more appropriate for a formal ball than an afternoon meeting. He was the king, and I would appear exactly as Sara decreed necessary. She knew better than I did, and after his comments about my hair last night—or had it been this morning?—I would do anything to avoid his ire. And to tell the truth, I was rapidly getting used to fine velvet and silk.

Still, my palms were sweating on said velvet as I curtsied in his office ten minutes later.

"I heard you were asking about the dungeon, my dear," he greeted me, leaning back in his chair.

Juliana. I could scarcely contain my fury, but at least I knew now who not to trust. That was valuable knowledge, even if I'd pay for it now.

"No, sire," I said, staring just over his shoulder. A painting hung on the wall behind his ornate desk, and I met the subject's gaze instead. A dead king was less intimidating. "Not really. Simply about the identity of the door—she was taking me on a tour."

"Is that so?" He stood and offered his arm. "Perhaps I was remiss in not doing the task myself. Juliana is quite competent, but your introduction to the castle should have been performed by someone more familiar."

"Sire, that's not necessary. I would not take you away from your duties." I couldn't imagine what those duties might be, but ledger upon ledger covered the top of his desk, along with a few rolled maps. Tyrant or not, his responsibilities must have been great.

"Nonsense," he replied, guiding me toward the door. "Welcoming you properly was my greatest duty, and I failed."

The guards outside fell in behind us, and I shut my mouth as we meandered through corridor after corridor in silence. Village girl or not, I wasn't naïve enough to not know where he was taking me. By the time we arrived at the barred door, my imagination had conjured up enough dismal outcomes to fill a library's worth of novels.

He didn't even need to order the guards to unlock the door. One did, then stepped back as he ushered me inside. We were alone in the corridor to the dungeon then, and against my better judgment, I clung to his arm as the door swung shut behind us, alerting everyone within hearing distance that someone had entered the dungeon.

"This was part of the original castle," he began in a conversational manner. I was beginning to understand that he fancied himself a storyteller, and had he been anyone else, I might have hung on his words—they were simply that powerful and intriguing. "Seven hundred years ago, when this place was nothing more than a hillside fortress, we didn't have the ability to store ice in the summer, so the basement was used for food storage. During one conflict or another, the cellars were repurposed for prisoners of war, and, eventually, our own criminals. Thieves, murderers—traitors."

"Fascinating," I murmured, though I was anything but fascinated. Apprehensive about seeing Thomas, that I was.

"Isn't it?" he asked. We reached the top of the

stairs, and his hold on me grew firmer, as though chivalry existed in a place like this. "Of course, its current use is rather unpleasant, and I'm afraid you're about to see some things that will shock a lady."

I steadied my knees. "I've seen hogs butchered."

He stared at me for a moment, then burst into laughter. The sound was impossibly loud in the closed stone stairwell, and I flinched, missing the last step. He grasped my elbow, and I somehow managed to find my feet on the slick floor.

Water—it had to be water I've just stepped in.

"These are not hogs here, my dear," he replied.

"Sire!" A rotund man hurried down the corridor to greet us, cutting off whatever else the king had planned to say. "You honor us with your presence." He shot a glance at me. "And the presence of your lady."

"A brief visit only, Hek. We're here to see one of your guests—Thomas Wennink."

I stiffened.

"Ah. He is—well, come, come."

He is what? I freed myself from King Laurent's hold and picked my way along the rough stone, stumbling the entire time. The dungeon was quieter than it was in my nightmares, but the smell of urine and mice was almost overpowering. There were no cells in the main corridor, but my quick glances to the left and right filled in the rest of the picture—any prisoners were down the hallways perpendicular to us, though I couldn't see much more than a few iron bars lit by a single torch.

"Here, here."

Hek motioned us left down the third cross-hallway, then stopped us before an arched doorway covered by bars. I blinked, trying to adjust to the darkness beyond them, but it was no use, even when Hek placed an oil torch in the holder outside.

"Thomas?" I called.

A scuffling sound came from within, then he appeared in the shadows deep inside.

"Riette?" More scuffling, then a curse. "What are you doing—" His eyes landed on my dress. "What are you wearing?"

He sounded weary but not broken, and my heart skipped a beat. Maybe he hadn't talked. Maybe the rest of his men were still safe. Maybe there was still hope.

"It's a long story," I said, still too close to the king. "The Feast of St. Margarethae—I'm to select a prisoner who deserves clemency."

There was a lengthy silence. I crept closer, lifting my skirts from the mud and water and heavens knew what else that flowed out of his cell through the channel drains on the floor outside. Childish infatuation or not, I badly wanted to reach in and touch him, but the chains around his ankles and neck prevented that—not to mention King Laurent's presence at my side.

"I've prayed for you since you were taken," I said, when he didn't reply. "For whatever that's worth." That was mostly a lie, but it sounded like something I was expected to say—by my parents, by the king, by God, by Thomas himself.

"That's enough for tonight, my dear." The king guided me backward with a light touch on my elbow. "The betrothal ball is tomorrow night, and you need your rest."

"Betrothal?" Thomas lunged at the bars, only to be brought up short by the length of the chain. In the dim of the dungeon I could see the delayed understanding in his eyes. "You—that dress? You wanted nice clothes and more food that badly?" He twisted toward the king. "You bastard. It's not enough for you to take our food and money. You have to take our women, too?"

I hadn't known King Laurent was carrying a sword. I should have noticed it earlier, but I'd been so distracted by the prospect of a visit to this horrid place that I hadn't paid attention to anything he was wearing. And if Thomas's reach didn't extend to the bars, the king's sword certainly reached inside. The point hit Thomas's neck, drawing a drop a blood.

"Questioning me is what got you here in the first place," the king snarled. "I would avoid any further missteps if you want to die with your tongue attached."

I held my breath. Interrupting this disagreement could be fatal; I certainly didn't want that sword under my throat. Thomas, after what seemed like an eternity, took a step back, and the king sheathed his sword once more.

"Good. At least you've learned something." He turned to me. "Come, Riette."

I wanted to kill him, or at least strike out at him. I could have struck him, too, because Hek had departed as soon as the king had drawn his sword. And even though he would overpower me almost immediately if I did, I was certainly the last person he'd expect to slap him or scream at him.

Instead, I meekly took his arm and walked out. There was only one thing left to do.

CHAPTER SEVEN

I DIDN'T KNOW WHAT THE APPROPRIATE ETIQUETTE WAS when greeting someone who had threatened to stab one of your friends. Thankfully, the man who'd done that was a king, so etiquette decided for me, just like it had decided on my gown, a deep ivory velvet that likely weighed more than its wearer.

Ignoring the stares of the hundred strangers crammed inside the throne room, I curtsied, then breathed a sigh of relief as he stood and offered his hand. As protocol demanded, I kissed the back of it, then took his arm. It was unnerving to be so close to someone who could kill me with a single move of his sword—or a single word—but it was either focus on him or the throng of eyes on me.

I chose him.

"I was beginning to think the castle was empty," I whispered as we proceeded out the throne room and into the ballroom. "Where did all these people come from?"

"Most of my advisors live elsewhere. Out of necessity. The courtiers too, for a long time now." If my breach of protocol in the form of speaking before the crowd irritated him, he didn't show it. "Perhaps someday . . ."

"What kind of necessity?" His wistfulness intrigued me.

"Shh." He placed a tender finger to my lips. "There will be no talk of politics tonight. This is a celebration."

Hardly offended by his completely logical reminder, I resisted the urge to turn back and stare at the crowd. "Do you ever get used to being the center of attention?"

"Never. If you could feel my heart, it would beat so quickly against your hand you'd think me ill." His lip turned up. "You just learn to live with it."

"Tell me how?"

He beamed at me as we passed through the grand doors. "You ask too much, my dear. Or at least, you ask for something I'm no expert in. You'll learn, same as we all do."

I wouldn't, but I couldn't say that, nor let on that my immediate future plans didn't include him. Etiquette —there was that word again—demanded we spend the evening together anyway, so I was stuck with him for now. There was, evidently, some tradition about proving to the people that we loved each other enough to spend a few hours together, even though our arrangement had nothing to do with affection, and everyone here knew it.

Juliana ran up to me as I was contemplating the horror of an upcoming dance with my new betrothed, wearing a gown which put my own to shame and clasping the hand of a young man whose blond curls were almost longer than her own. She curtsied for the king and nodded at me, then smiled.

"Sire, if you don't mind the interruption, I've been wanting to introduce Riette to Berend since she arrived."

King Laurent's brows rose. "Berend. You've returned from Braunitz later than scheduled."

Juliana shot me a look. *The king controls the conversation*, she seemed to say. *You'll get used to it.*

"Snowmelt made the Kalcine impassable for almost a week," Juliana's companion replied. "We finally managed to ford it just a few days ago—it was a difficult ride back."

"I'm glad you made it when you did. Juliana has told you of my news?"

"She has." To his credit, the man turned toward me, including me at last. "And I wish both you all the happiness we've found."

I smothered a giggle. *Happiness.* Did we all play the same game, or were he and Juliana truly content together? She was staring up at the young man like he was the only person in the room, so perhaps they were. Jealousy replaced my amusement. I would never find that. Not with King Laurent, my betrothal vow being the lie it was. Maybe not even with Thomas.

"Thank you." King Laurent drew my hand up and kissed it. "Berend, this is Riette. Riette, the Duke of Athnard, Juliana's husband."

Juliana was married to a duke? That explained much. With flushed cheeks, I gave him a short curtsy, acutely aware that a week before we'd never have been standing in the same room, and he wouldn't have bothered speaking to me.

"I'm so pleased to meet you, Your Grace. Juliana has been quite welcoming. She's made my transition as pleasant as it can be."

"She doesn't argue when I choose her clothes, and that's good enough for me. It's almost like dressing a doll." Juliana sidled up to me and favored King

Laurent with what I felt was an overly intimate, pleading expression. "Please, dear brother, might I borrow her for just a while?"

My breath caught.

Brother?

I hadn't been aware of the certain angle of their chins before, but it was there, along with the same long, dark lashes that had caught my attention when I'd first met the king. They'd looked incongruous underneath Juliana's blonde curls, but it now it was all too clear they'd both inherited the look—probably from the man hanging on the wall in the king's office.

"You know the rules. Betrothal festivities." Her husband chuckled before King Laurent could respond. "And I have missed dancing with my wife."

I gave her an apologetic look as he dragged her off, leaving me alone with the king once more. "Juliana's your sister," I said. "I had no idea."

"Younger by seven years." He gave her a look at she walked away, and I suspected he'd barely avoided rolling his eyes. "A former handful, she was."

"A family trait, sire?" Heavens, had I just flirted with him?

Surprise flashed across his face, like I'd just accused him of something worse than treason, then faded into amusement. "No. Not exactly. Though I suspect I was a disappointment to my father in other ways."

It was the wrong time and wrong place to ask him why—for that matter, I doubted questioning his comment would ever be appropriate. Still, it stabbed at my mind, breaking loose curiosity I didn't know I had. I knew his father had died when I was a toddler, his regent had been an uncle who'd died ten years ago, but I had little knowledge in the way the Meirdrean court had worked when he was a child. Growing up in a village on the moors didn't help with that.

"I'm sorry to hear that," I replied.

"Ancient history. We all make do with the situations we find ourselves in today."

I was about to open my mouth to reply when a brilliant glare caught my gaze, like the light of our fireplace had reflected off the coin in Willem's hand that night. Fire? My heart skipped a beat, but there seemed to be no panic in the ballroom to suggest such. I turned toward the light, and as I did, it focused itself on a single spot on the floor.

On the spot due west of Lochfeld.

I rubbed my eyes, and King Laurent caught me gently by the forearm. "My dear, are you quite well? You've gone pale."

I looked up and down the ballroom, mostly filled

with velvet and silk. Outside of the hundreds of candles that illuminated the space, nothing else glowed. It was the diamonds I'd seen, and Juliana hadn't, the sparkling that I'd blamed on the headache the crown had given me.

The crown . . .

"No. I'm fine. It's just—your map. It—" I shook my head and twisted my wrist from him. I couldn't confess to what I was seeing. He'd think me mad, would send me from the castle at once, and then Thomas's fate would be sealed. "It's beautiful."

"If only I had the ability to create something so lovely, I could die happy. But it brought you to me, you know."

"How?"

"I threw a coin." He grinned, somehow shy. "It landed on Elternow without rolling, so I sent Willem there to select a wife."

Becoming a king's bride because of a coin toss was more than a little amusing. He led me onward, introducing me to advisors and dukes and counts—all the while smiling graciously as I floundered about, pretending this was somewhere I belonged, feigning that I couldn't wait to become an official member of the court. In truth, I wanted out of this ballroom and away from its maddening map, and I wanted out of the castle.

By the time he pulled me into an alcove and offered me a small glass of wine, my feet were sore, my head was beginning to ache from the cacophony of a hundred voices in an enclosed space, and my soul ached to examine the wood floor. In short, both my body and mind were failing me. Our token privacy might have the slightest hint of impropriety to it, but no one would question the king needing time with his betrothed, and I needed the break. Settling on the bench there, I moved my toes back and forth in their silk prisons until the blood began to flow again.

"You've done wonderfully tonight." He traced a finger down my cheek. "I am so very lucky they went to your house first."

His touch made me shiver like Thomas's kisses once had, and I hated him for that. "I'm pleased I've done right by you, sire."

"You certainly have." His smile slipped. "I know you don't love me now. But could you ever?"

It was the last thing I'd expected him to say when he'd escorted me over here. The alcove, though open to the ballroom, became a sweltering furnace, and I was certain he could feel my unwelcome reaction. I lowered my gaze to my shoes, but there was no way he took that for demureness, either.

"I wasn't aware a fondness for each other was a prerequisite for a royal marriage," I replied.

Or any marriage.

He sat back and examined me. "My parents did not love one another. Can you imagine what it's like to grow up watching that? To wonder if that would be you one day? To wish you could find something more?"

"No," I said quietly. My parents had loved each other—for the most part. Marrying for love wasn't common in their generation either, though sometimes I believed they'd grown into their love. "I can't."

"Juliana found happiness. My mother has at long last, even though it's in another kingdom. And I wish the same for myself." I didn't reply, and he coughed, once. "But I'm aware such things can take time. I won't rush you."

"Sire!"

A man in a cream and navy uniform—cavalry, I thought it might be—darted toward us, and the king stood, his forehead creasing in concern as his fingers brushed mine.

"Lieutenant? I trust you're not interrupting my respite to discuss strategy."

The lieutenant bowed rapidly, more out of breath

than he should have been from an evening on a ball-room floor. "Sire, we've just received word from our scouts of Nantoisens skulking near Vilstel. They've crossed the border!"

I glanced up, alarmed. Vilstel was a fishing port, and an important one at that. We'd never traded with them, but much of the kingdom did, and an attack on the shipping and fish markets there would be devastating.

The king waved his hand. "Another raid. It's as if they know we're otherwise occupied this week."

"Not just a raid this time." The lieutenant's lips thinned. "They destroyed sixteen ships two days ago. The people are frightened, riots are beginning. If left unchecked—"

"I see." King Laurent's face had gone grave, and a small cluster of questioning men in uniform had surrounded us. "You've saddled Foxfire?"

The lieutenant nodded.

"Riette." The king turned to me and gave the slightest nod of his chin. "I'm afraid I must ride tonight. Some things must be taken care of in person. I'm sorry to delay to our nuptials, but another few days will seem like an hour in the end."

He kissed my hand, and as Juliana took his place

and patted away what she doubtlessly thought should be tears, I celebrated inside.

I had at least three days to figure out a way to free Thomas.

And find out why the map on the ballroom floor was glowing in the exact place where the Nantoisen raiders had crossed the border.

CHAPTER EIGHT

JULIANA FELL TO HER KNEES BESIDE ME IN THE EMPTY ballroom, a look of skepticism on her face.

"You had a headache, Riette," she said. "Even the surgeon said it can sometimes cause vision disturbances. Just like you described—shimmers and sparkles and wavy lines. You ought to know that as well"

I could hear the doubt of my healing abilities in her tone, and maybe she was right. "The headache ended when we stepped inside here—and my sight became better. It was only this small piece that sparkled."

I brushed my fingertips over the wood of the Meirdrean-Nantoise border, but it was dark, like the rest of the outline. The diamond-like glitter that had drawn my attention before was gone, and as much as I blinked and rubbed my eyes, it refused to reappear.

"And it's not now?" she asked.

I knelt back. "It's not now. And I don't understand."

"You were seeing things." Her admonition was kind but firm. "You just needed rest, and no one would blame you for that."

"Maybe." I had less desire to argue—or even speak with her—now that I knew she was the king's sister.

"Well," she replied, pushing herself to her feet, "I'm in need of some fresh air. Would you care to join me for a stroll through the east garden?"

I shook my head. A thin layer of snow had fallen last night, and my body hadn't yet forgotten what *too cold* felt like.

"I think I'll retire for a few hours. You're right— maybe I just need some rest."

Juliana didn't argue, and once she'd stepped outside the ballroom, I second-guessed my desire for a nap. After a few days' time, I would never have the chance to visit a castle again. Perhaps my new surroundings had sparked a hitherto undiscovered sense of adventure. The east passage from the ballroom led to the stairwell that would take me straight to my room, so I chose the west corridor, narrower and dark in the late afternoon, yet still lit with the ubiquitous oil lamps. The stone walls eventually opened up into a small courtyard

which was probably lovely in every other season. Today
the walls blocked nearly the entire sun, and I shivered
as I hurried across, cursing my decision to not bring a
cloak.

So intent was I of reaching shelter that I didn't see
the patch of ice until it was too late. My elbow
slammed into the stone first, followed by my hip. I lay
there for a moment, stunned beyond words, until the
chill of melted snow began to seep through my bodice.

Soaked.

I pushed myself to my feet, finding yet another
injury as I did so. My ankle refused to hold my weight,
so I leaned against the nearest wall and lifted my gown
just enough to see a brilliant red mark under my
stocking that was sure to become a bruise. Too bad I
couldn't do much about it without the stash of herbs I'd
left in Elternow.

"This certainly wasn't the way I expected to meet
his betrothed."

I dropped my skirts and screeched. The owner of
the voice—who'd now seen more of my leg than was
proper—was dressed in black robes and carried a half
dozen leather-bound books under his arm. His attire
gave him away at once, and no matter that religion had
been an afterthought in a village where growing food
was more important than anything else, I was just pious

enough to be humiliated at the predicament he'd found me in.

"It's strange," he began, helping me stand with his free hand, "how many react to my appearance with that very reaction."

A flushed spread across my cheeks, the only warm thing in the courtyard. "I slipped on the ice, Father. My ankle is—not broken, I would think, but I'm not sure I can make it back to my room."

Not up all those stairs.

"Lucky for you that I was a physician before joining the church. Yours is not the first ankle I've seen, nor will it be the last, I'm sure." The corners of his eyes crinkled. "I lit the fire in the library an hour ago, and it must be blazing by now. Please, come warm up. You appear to need it."

I hobbled inside, fully intending on finding the closest chair to said fireplace—but froze in astonishment once we crossed the threshold. The castle had impressed me from the first hour, with its silken walls and arched ceilings and marble floors, but the library was something out of a dream.

Ornate rugs lay on the wood floor, tempering their high polish. Several brocade chairs were clustered around the fireplace, a typical arrangement for this time of year—likely they'd be moved to the overhang outside in spring. The ceiling was carved in the same style as the throne room, but this time I could pick out the stories told in the mahogany and ebony: fairy tales. Princes and kings who wielded magical swords, malicious ghouls who made deals with malevolent fairies, princesses who saved their land from evil.

And the books? It wasn't difficult to tear my stare from the ceiling. I'd never seen so many. Had never imagined so many existed in the entire kingdom.

The priest helped me to a chair, and I fell gratefully into it, thankful for the ability to take weight off my sore ankle. His books hit a table somewhere behind me, then he appeared again, this time with a tumbler of clear fluid.

"Oh," I said. "Thank you, but I couldn't possibly—"

"Medicinal," he replied, taking a seat next to me. "If anyone bothers you about it, tell them I ordered it."

Whatever liquor he'd poured burned my throat going down, but a pleasant warm sensation welled up in my chest, and I decided he was right. Melted snow soaked the hem of my gown, my left sleeve in not much better shape, but until I warmed enough to stand the feel of ice on my bare foot in private, I wasn't going anywhere. Fire and liquor, it was.

"So," he went on, "you were it."

I didn't have to ask what he meant. The story of my arrival must have been going around the castle for days.

"Yes." I sucked down the rest of the glass and set it aside. "I must confess, though, we don't learn of these royal traditions where I'm from. I was shocked to find the king chooses a bride from the nearby villages."

"Did he explain why?"

I flushed again, hoping he'd blame it on the flames and drink. "Yes."

"All of it?"

"I'm not sure what you're implying, Father . . ."

"Gerritt Rasch. But Gerritt will do." He gave me a quiet smile and crossed an ankle over his knee. "Meirdre's troubles are nothing new. Our location between the Lisdee Mountains and the sea puts us in an excellent—and precarious—position in this part of the world, and this narrow plain on which we exist doesn't help matters. Good, heavy rainfall, ideal for crops and livestock, plus access to the open ocean which allows for fishing and trade. Some would prefer not to trade, instead taking what they want without giving us compensation in return."

I raised my eyebrows. "You're a teacher as well as a priest and physician?" I asked skeptically.

"Just setting the stage." He peered at me oddly, like he knew a secret. "Border raids turn to skirmishes, skirmishes turn to battles, battles turn to all-out wars. Seventeen were killed in the village of Granbar last month over their grain stores. I'm afraid it'll get worse before it gets better."

I shivered, but it had to be my damp clothing. "We've always been insulated from the border raids in Elternow. I didn't realize it was so bad."

"The king does. He might be a difficult man— believe me, I know he's hardly someone to hold up as the paradigm of virtue—but he cares what happens to this kingdom and its people."

A noncommittal sound rose in my throat, eased onward, I supposed, by the liquor.

The priest laughed out loud. "Oh, he adores his power as well. Thankfully, that works in all of our favors. It behooves him to keep his borders secure and his people safe and happy—relatively so."

Did he know his king had a rebel locked in an arctic dungeon not so far away from where we sat in front of a blazing fire? None of us in Meirdre were safe. Happy? Well, that was debatable. I wasn't unhappy exactly, but anxious for the future? Yes.

"I can see you disagree with much of what I've said. No matter." He stared into the flames for a long time. "Back to why the king needed to marry a common woman, then."

"I think we've established why."

"Not entirely. Your parents have always been farmers?"

"Yes."

"And you were born and grew up in the meadows of Elternow."

"Yes." I drew out the word.

"Hmmm." He stared at me, a finger on his cheek. "Then there's a chance you're a crownkeeper."

My forehead creased in what was probably a most disagreeable manner. I'd never heard of such a thing, and it sounded vaguely superstitious and nonsensical. But he looked serious, so I forced the same expression to my face.

"I don't know what that is."

"Most don't." Father Gerritt tapped his fingers on a book on the table between us. "For reasons which will soon become apparent. You've seen the map in the ballroom, of course."

The question made me wish for another drink. "Of course."

"Well, then . . . every so often, a child is born with a particular connection to Creation. Several a year, in fact, though they usually go unknown, unaware of their gift. It benefits our sovereign to choose one of these women, even if most times, they do not."

Maps, peasant children, the king's choice of a bride. It made no sense.

"But why?" I asked.

"There is an additional gift granted to these children, bestowed upon their marriage. Or coronation, in the case of monarchs in their right, though I know of no cases where a royal child has been born with the necessary bond. They're referred to as crownkeepers—but only in private, you understand. They can feel when Meirdre is in danger, can warn of wildfires, border raids, epidemics. And the map speaks to them, shows them where misfortune is happening."

My eyes grew wide. "But that's witchcraft!"

He chuckled. "Hardly. Who do you think bestows that gift upon them? The evil one cares not for protecting something he only seeks to destroy."

I moaned in dismay. It all sounded . . . too coincidental?

"Why so disheartened?" he asked. "Most would be flattered to be granted a gift like this—and truthfully, I may be explaining this to you for no reason at all. We have no way of knowing if you're one of these children until you're wed."

"Father—" Did I dare speak of what Juliana and I had done? I didn't want to, but I could still see the undulating lines in the ballroom when I closed my eyes.

"If I confess something, you'll keep it in confidence? Even to the king?"

He spread his hands. "Naturally."

I took a deep breath.

And then I told him about the map.

CHAPTER NINE

FOR THE NEXT DAY, I WAS IN SUCH KNOTS ABOUT Father Gerritt's revelation that I scarcely thought of Thomas. When I wasn't in the chapel pleading to be released from this unwanted power, I was in the ballroom, forcing Juliana to teach me the dances I'd be expected to know on my wedding day. Thankfully, I was becoming a rather accomplished actress, and she had no idea of my true intentions. The map refused to glow again, however, and I constantly questioned the things Father Gerritt had told me. Had I slipped on the ice that day, hit my head, and imagined it all?

Earlier this afternoon, she had ridden off with her duke husband, making an excuse about needing sunshine and fresh air. I'd sat in my room embroidering for three hours before the light had become bad and my back stiff. It was becoming a routine of sorts, and I was grateful for anything that reminded me of home and took my mind off . . . whatever I'd turned into. A princess, a monster? I didn't know. Thomas was no doubt furious I was living in luxury, and my parents would be frightened of this new power I'd found.

And the king—Juliana's brother, I kept reminding myself—would have me hung if he knew my plans.

Later that afternoon, I found myself before the door to the dungeon, anyway, having cornered a sentry on the way down. I'd picked a young and nervous one, too, to verify my story with Captain Willem. I'd told him that the king had allowed me to bring a prisoner some food and gave him my best fake smile, though I was cringing inside. Flirting had never been a strength of mine, even when the first part of my plan depended on it.

"I'm so glad you could escort me," I said, peering through the bars. "The king will be relieved to know everyone in the castle is being so helpful."

"It's no issue at all, uh . . ." He trailed off, perhaps realizing he had no idea what to call me.

"Riette." My smile faltered, and I waved toward the door. "Can we get this over with? I'm anxious about going down and just want to be back up as soon as I can."

He nodded, practically falling over himself in an effort to unlock it. "I'll be waiting here when you get back. Good luck—and make sure you stay far away from those cells." His eyes widened. "They can grab you, even from inside."

"I'll keep that in mind," I whispered. I was only after Thomas, but if anyone else occupied those cells . . . yes, that worried me.

The hair on my forearms rose as I descended the stairs where the king had led me just a few days before. I popped a dried strawberry from the basket in my mouth, desperate for the tang to cure the dryness which had taken up permanent residence around my tongue. The sourness worked, and focusing on it allowed me to walk the rest of the way without panicking at the sound of weeping coming from somewhere farther below.

"Miss Riette?" Hek's question boomed off the stone walls as he approached; in the background, the weeping became louder. "What in the heavens are you doing here?"

I lifted the basket and prepared to lie once more. "In honor of our betrothal and the Feast of St. Margaretha, the king has asked me to bring these down so the prisoners might be able to see a taste of what they are missing because of their crimes."

Hek's broad face broke into a smile. "And you

volunteered so you might speak to one of them alone before his execution, yes?"

"I—"

"You have nothing to fear from what he's confessed here. We know you refused to be a part of his treachery. He said you would have turned him in had you had the chance."

Thomas had protected me? Through torture?

Well, of course he had. Making these kinds of decisions, even during his own suffering, was why he'd risen to his position.

"I did." I forced a modest expression. "I am loyal to our king."

"He must love you to protect you after all that."

"He must," I murmured, understanding we were talking about Thomas again, though I wondered if that was true. Thomas was more about duty and loyalty than anything else—though I supposed there were some feelings there somewhere. "Can I speak with him?"

Hek reached for the basket. "Second corridor, turn left, fourth cell. Five minutes."

I relinquished the dried berries and crept off down the stone tunnel, my heart thumping. What was I supposed to say to Thomas? *I'm planning to get you out of here?* If they tortured him again before murdering him, he might not be able to keep my secret again, and then we'd both be dead.

The thought of standing on top of the scaffolding overcame me, and I stopped to rest my forehead against the cool wall. Mildew. Blood. Urine. Focusing on the smells that washed over me didn't do anything to block my fears, nor the crying which had turned to moans.

What am I supposed to do?

Whatever it was, leaning against a wall wasn't it.

Mustering all of my courage, I proceeded to Thomas's cell. There was no torch here as there'd been before, and it was only the light from the main corridor which allowed me to remain on my feet. Clumsy I was not, but the uneven stone would make even a swan ungainly, and my sore ankle didn't help matters. At the fourth cell, identifiable only because it was darker than where I stood, I stopped.

"Thomas?"

Something shifted beyond the bars at my whisper, then moaned.

"Riette? What are you—"

"Shush. I only have five minutes, and we need to talk about getting you out of here."

"Getting me out? Don't tell me you have some sort of plan."

"No," I admitted, pressing my face against the bars and squinting into the darkness. "But I have hairpins. I wasn't sure I'd even get this far, so—"

"Toss me one. Just straight forward. I'll find it."

I pulled one from my hair and did so. A rattling echoed from inside—shackles releasing? I glanced frantically behind me, certain the noise would bring guards, but the corridor remained empty. Rattling shackles, I realized, weren't given a second thought down here.

Thomas appeared at the bars a moment later, his rough palms on my cheeks. The touch of his icy hands was chilling, but I didn't pull away—he'd doubtless been through enough that seeing and feeling another human who didn't intend him harm was more healing than anything else I could do.

"I've missed you," he whispered.

"I've missed you, too."

I'd have kissed him had we had more space between the bars. As it was, I squeezed his hand, luxuriating in the sensation of his calluses. They meant something—that he was still the same boy who'd climbed trees with me as a child and helped Papa with the plowing and taught me basic swordsmanship.

He picked the lock to his cell with his free hand as I remembered the weight of that first sword in my hand, and before I could protest that we had more urgent matters, his lips were against mine. I kissed him back, though Hek's return was at the front of my mind.

"Sorry." He tucked the pin back in my hair. "I needed to do that before anything else."

I grinned at him. "I'm not complaining. But Thomas—I wasn't planning on breaking you out today."

"Have to take the chances as they come," he said, pushing me behind him. "There may not be another. You gave me a way out of the shackles and this cell, and that's not something I thought I'd see when I woke up earlier. What time is it?"

"I don't know," I stammered. "Late afternoon, I suppose. Or early evening."

My heart fell. He was going to try to run, and I couldn't see him hurt.

Silly girl. Would you rather see him swinging?

"Then you have wonderful timing." He gave me another kiss on my cheek, and I didn't fight that one, either. "An escape at dark is what I've been dreaming of."

"But I have no plan. King Laurent is still gone, but—"

"That's all right. Just turn around and walk out. I'll take care of everything else."

He sounded casual. Too casual. Was it possible he

never meant to walk out of here at all? Had he decided to martyr himself in this dungeon, to become an inspiration for whoever was willing to follow him?

I wanted to ask, but as I tiptoed toward the main corridor, the light grew brighter, and Hek and whatever other guards roamed the dungeon would hear anything I said. I kept my head up and a light smile on my face, wondering what he was up to.

Until a dagger pressed across my throat.

CHAPTER TEN

I GASPED OUT LOUD AS THE WEIGHT OF THE COOL BLADE settled against my skin, and Thomas laughed.

"That's right. Just keep walking, girl. Slowly now. Keep your hands in front of you and don't struggle."

His voice was icy, and I understood at once. I slowed, both to give him another few moments to prepare and to slow my own racing heart. Hek must have heard, for boots echoed at the end of the corridor —several sets. He'd brought guards.

"Back off! Unless you'd like to explain to your king," Thomas hollered at him, "why his betrothed's blood is coating the floor of this place."

"You won't escape." Hek didn't back away, but his sword lowered a fraction. I was more worried about the three guards behind him whose swords didn't move.

"You can't let him get away," I added lamely. A skilled actress, I was not.

Thomas pinched the back of my arm through layers of fabric. I flinched, then shut my mouth. I could take a hint.

"You could have waited, Wennink!" The shout was louder than before. "Rumor was that you were to be released in celebration of the feast."

"Is that true?" Thomas asked under his breath.

I froze, and he crashed into my back. I'd already told him this. What was he playing at now?

"No," I replied quietly. "They're lying."

The truth would have to come later. Thomas would be furious I'd kept important information from him, but if it mattered that much to him, he should have asked for all the details before he kissed me and put a knife to my throat.

"I thought as much. Wouldn't expect anything else from the king's men." He stopped us just short of striking distance. "I'm walking out of here with her. One of you"—he pointed—"will proceed us. I want a horse. I was riding by the time I turned two, so don't try to stick with me a lame one. She comes with me. I'll leave her on the trail halfway down the cliff. Unharmed."

Hek shifted from foot to foot. "I can't agree to that."

The point of the dagger turned inward, and I squeaked in shock. Thomas knew better than to rely on my acting talent. If I didn't trust him so implicitly, I'd have been terrified.

"If the rumor you spoke of was true, you have nothing to fear by letting me go, do you?" Thomas asked. "I'm simply earning my freedom a bit early."

"And hers? You will guarantee she'll return?" Hek called.

"You'll have to take that chance I won't need a hostage for long." Thomas smirked. I couldn't see him, but I could hear it in his voice.

"That's not what I mean." Hek sheathed his sword and held his hands out to his sides. "She may prefer to follow you, and you understand that I can't allow that."

Yes, yes, I do!

"She'd be a fool to follow someone who doesn't love her," Thomas said, pushing me forward once more. I stumbled on an uneven stone, and he yanked me up so hard I cried out. "I don't think you have anything to worry about there."

At least one of us could act.

The unarmed guard who led us through the castle fulfilled his duty well. He followed the more remote passageways and knew which chambers would be empty, and where we would encounter servants instead of soldiers and guards. I stumbled along, Thomas's feet a continual hazard, and by the time we reached the ballroom, my sore ankle was aching once more.

"Thomas," I gasped. "We have to stop."

"No."

He pushed me forward, through the open doors. I tripped and limped behind the guard, focusing on my feet—and then something else.

A glowing piece of wood.

Regardless of what Thomas wanted, I stopped. The glowing area wasn't an area of the kingdom I knew, but he wasn't going to wait for me to call for Juliana and have a conversation about geography. It was near the castle, yes. Between Elternow and where we stood atop these cliffs. West of the Arsele Forest, east of the Kalcine River.

Thomas pushed me forward once more, toward a door on the long end of the ballroom, and I ignored everything but the map. Committing to memory what I had seen seemed important, and I mentally recited the location over and over as the guard led us into a court-yard where official visitors stabled their rides. Whether

I'd remember it in an hour was another story, but since I couldn't tell the king, I could tell Thomas—he'd help.

The guard pointed to a chestnut stallion, saddled and apparently docile. Thomas nodded—the horse looked like any other horse to me, but he'd seen something in the animal that met with his approval, and I didn't argue. He looked like he was capable of carrying both of us back to Elternow, and that was all I needed to know.

Well, that and what was going on in that piece of land near the castle, between Elternow and where we stood atop these cliffs, west of the Arsele forest, east of the Kalcine river.

"Riette!" Juliana dashed toward us in her riding clothes, flushed and sweating, even in the cooling evening air. "What's going on? I heard such a commotion—" She focused on the dagger in Thomas's hand. "Who is this man? Has he harmed you?"

"Juliana," I managed to stutter, "I'm sorry."

And I was. She'd been kind to me. She couldn't help who her brother was.

Her eyes widened. I couldn't tell if she had any idea what was going on, but she darted toward me, her skirts flying. The guard moved to grab her, and Thomas, taking the opportunity, pushed me up on the saddle, then jumped up behind me with a shout to the horse.

Hooves flew. I grabbed the pommel with my finger-tips. Thomas wound a hand around my waist, and for the first time since I'd come to the castle, I felt secure.

Confident.

Safe.

Behind me, Thomas gave a shout, and then we were gone.

He slowed the stallion to a trot as soon as we entered the woods below the cliffs. The trail was wide—used by the army as it was—but the cover surrounding us was heavy. No one seemed to be pursuing us, and for the moment, we could breathe easier. I leaned back against him, trying to adjust for my poor seat.

"Thomas, we've got to find another horse for me. I'm afraid he's not going to make it much farther carrying both of us."

Thomas whistled at the drenched stallion, and we came to a halt in a clearing, obviously created to make use of the spring to our left. Yawning, he slid from the saddle and tossed the reins in my lap. For a man who'd spent a while in a dungeon, he didn't look bad—he'd lost weight, yes, but he appeared lithe rather than sick. His beard wasn't scraggly in the least, and while the breeches he'd likely been wearing since he'd been arrested were dirty, they weren't covered in the blood I'd feared.

"You're going back," he said. "I'll walk. Rorswil isn't far, and I can pick up another mount there."

"Go back?" I twisted toward him and flicked the reins, enough to let the horse circle and catch his breath.

"You are to marry King Laurent, are you not?"

The stallion and I circled around him twice.

"Of course not," I said with all the courage I could muster. "I had no intention of doing so. Well, perhaps at first, when they told me what the marriage would do for Mama and Papa, but once we arrived at Lochfeld and I realized you were down below . . . I always meant to leave with you."

Thomas threw back his head and laughed. "You don't love me, Riette."

It was a slap, just like I'd felt back in the dungeon. "If we're going to make those accusations, I would think you're the guilty one, Thomas." The horse's ears flicked nervously at my sharp tone.

"Well, you're right about that. You didn't think I'd settle down and marry you, did you?"

I yanked on the reins harder than I should have and the horse gave a snort. The words were heavy. I *had* thought that. Of course Thomas would grow weary of fighting a never-ending battle. I had assumed he'd slink off to another village, another kingdom, one where he wasn't known, and that we'd begin our new lives together. After rescuing my parents from Laurent's wrath, of course. The feelings we had for each other were enough. We would grow to love each other in time, and if we didn't? Our history together would be enough to bind us in mutual respect, and even if it never turned to love, *that* would be enough.

Wouldn't it?

The question—and the answer I didn't want to admit to myself—exhausted me. I leaned forward against the horse's neck and closed my eyes.

"Heavens, Riette, you did." Thomas appeared at my side. "I had no idea. I never meant—"

"How many men do you think I've kissed?" I asked, digging my fingers into the horse's mane. He must have been well-trained, for he did nothing but snort and toss and his head.

"I never gave it any thought, truthfully."

"One. You, Thomas. It was just you." I made a sound of frustration, and the stallion snorted again. Nervous he was not, but my anger was bothering him. "I thought we had an understanding. I thought we had a future!"

He looked up at me, steady as he could be. "My loyalty is to Meirdre and her people. There is no room for anything else."

His claim slammed into me, almost unseating me. Even though we'd just agreed we didn't love each other, I could scarcely believe what he'd said. I could scarcely believe what I'd *heard*. The reins loosened in my hands, and the horse, freed from the pressure, began to paw at the ground.

Thomas caught him by the bridle. "I care for you. But being saddled with a wife isn't something I can do now. Likely not ever."

My cheeks grew red, even in the chilled air—then the rest of me followed, hot and trembling, as I realized he was right. What else was there for someone like me? We grew up—if we were lucky—we married, we had babies, we strive to provide enough food for all, we grew old, we died. In Meirdre, no one of our status ever dared to hope for more.

"I never wanted you like that." My reply was childish, but I wanted to hurt him as much as he'd hurt me.

"Riette . . . we're going to pretend?" His hand fell on top of mine. "Even now?"

I dug my heels into the stallion's side. He reared, and Thomas took a step back. Into a mud puddle, I was glad to see.

"What else do you expect me to say?" I asked.

"I don't know." He sighed. "You won't go back?"

"To marry that man? Never."

"Then where? I can't just let you ride aimlessly about the countryside—and think of your parents! What do you think he'll do to them when he finds out you're gone?"

"We'll leave Elternow. He won't search for us forever." The idea of King Laurent finding Mama and Papa and me made me want to curl up and die in terror. "He can't."

"Riette." His chin fell to his chest. "I can't let you do that."

"You—" I gave a little pressure on the reins. "You have no authority over me."

"That doesn't mean I don't care about you."

I brought the horse to a halt, more to show Thomas I had some skills than anything else. "Prove it."

"Prove it? Even if I was able to—"

"I need you to take me somewhere," I interrupted.

"Where?"

I closed my eyes and spouted off the directions I'd memorized. "Between Elternow and where we stood atop these cliffs. West of the Arsele forest, east of the Kalcine river."

"That's an interesting way of giving directions." He

narrowed his eyes at me. "But that's Haszen. Got to be."

"Fine," I said, reaching down a hand in invitation. "Then take me to Haszen."

Haszen.

Near the castle, between Elternow and the cliffs, west of the Arsele forest, east of the Kalcine river.

I repeated the words over and over as we trotted down the footpath. Thomas had only agreed to throw any pursuers off our trail—of that I was certain. They'd expect him to head for his woods near Rorswil, but we'd turned west, out of the woods. No hoofbeats followed us as we headed through a vast countryside of rolling hills that seemed to stretch forever in every direction. In the summer they'd likely be as green as the emeralds in what would have been my crown, but now they were dead. Brown. Crisp. Several haystacks sat at the top of few of the hills, and even from this distance, they were black.

"Soldiers burned them." Thomas spoke for the first time since we'd rested the horse a half hour ago. "Soon as they were stacked."

"Why?" My voice was a whisper.

"Starve the people and their livestock and they can't rebel." His bitterness carried on the icy wind that whipped around us. "Maybe you did the right thing by not going back."

"It looks like mold." I squinted at the haystacks, then at the river in the distance, spilling out of its banks even in the middle of the winter. "Lots of rain here."

"It was fire," he snapped. "You can tell by the color."

I couldn't, but his tone bade no argument.

"I'm afraid," I said, changing the subject. "Something's going to happen in Haszen. I—I feel it somehow."

"Reprisals?" he asked sharply.

Was his rebellion the only thing he thought about?

"I don't know," I admitted. Why wasn't the cursed map color-coded? "It's just a feeling. Perhaps if we could ride about town a bit, see if anything looks unusual—"

"No." His reply was piercing. "There's a house where we'll be protected. We'll hide out there for now and figure out what to do next. I may have to take a side trip to Elternow and make sure your parents are safe before we head that way."

"Thomas—"

I was trapped. Father Gerritt had made one thing

clear—the enchantment of the map was a secret. I couldn't speak of it to Thomas lest he laugh at me and call me silly, but I couldn't search an entire town alone, either. I wasn't *meant* to. No queen could protect the entire kingdom—but she could pass down valuable information and let others do the foot work.

And because I'd left Lochfeld, I'd have to figure it out alone.

We fell into silence then, shivering as the horse slowed to walk on the hard ground. We'd been pushing the stallion too hard, but the deepening clouds to the north spoke of more snow. Being caught in the hillside when it came could be life-threatening.

And Haszen was hours away.

CHAPTER ELEVEN

BY THE TIME WE RODE INTO HASZEN, THE FLURRIES
danced around us, and despite the snow, my eyes were
wide. Compared to Elternow, the town was sprawling.
I'd never imagined a church so tall, or houses so close
together, or streets without the stray horse or cow. A
fortress sat upon the hill to the north, crumbling with
disuse, and as we trotted across a wooden footbridge
over a thin, frozen stream, bells rang.

The entire scene was enough to warm my soul, if
not my body.

Thomas brought the stallion to a stop outside a
house on the end of a low row of buildings. The timber
door was worn and scratched, but smoke rose from the
four chimneys. I shivered as the warmth of his body left
me, and I could not follow him inside quickly enough.

Somehow, I'd expected an inn, but when I shook off the little snow that had settled on my head and looked around, I realized it was a private home. That made sense—if Thomas was wanted in Haszen, this was safer. I didn't particularly care what we were doing here, because the fire across the room was roaring, the meager table in between was set with wine and bread, and my fingers were already thawing. Figures moved somewhere in my corner vision, but I was too focused on the fire to pay them any heed.

"Thomas." A man's voice broke through the chill that still hung about me. "Wasn't expecting to see you here. Or at all, truthfully. Who's the girl?"

"This is Riette." Thomas shrugged off the cloak he'd stolen from a barn hours before, and I turned toward the man he was speaking to.

"Strange," came the reply. "Riette is the name of Laurent's new betrothed."

It was the first time I'd heard someone speak the king's name with such utter casualness. The speaker was older than Thomas, perhaps closer to Papa's age, his scraggly gray hair almost shoulder-length. Fine— some didn't have time for hygiene. But it was the way he held himself, as if he expected to spring toward anyone at any second, that set my teeth on edge. Well, that and the fact he'd somehow put together my appearance and Thomas's escape with nary a question or confusion.

"She had a hairpin." Thomas glanced at me, then nodded. "She's from Elternow. We grew up together."

No mention of any relationship. I couldn't determine what that meant.

"You trust her?"

"Yes."

"Hmm."

The man stared at me, and in my gown, I felt like he was seeing someone I wasn't. A woman who belonged in another world, one with silk sheets and dungeons and ballroom floors that sparkled. How was I supposed to convince him that wasn't me? That I might have lived there for a time, but my body and mind belonged somewhere else? Heavens, my fingers were still callused from milking, and the dress I've chosen because Juliana was away from the castle was hardly the height of fashion.

"She should go upstairs," he went on.

I hadn't realized there were people higher in the rebellion than Thomas, but this man's tone left no room for doubt. With a slight smile, I headed upstairs, wrapping the blanket around myself as the warmth of the kitchen turned to ice in the stairwell. But there was a fireplace in the first room I found, and it only took a bit of effort to light a small fire with what little wood remained inside.

It was no royal bedroom in a castle, but after riding for a long while through the frozen meadows of Meirdre, it might as well have been. The mattress on the floor smelled like fresh hay, and even though there was a small pile of screws in the corner which spoke of the fate of the bed, I collapsed on it, exhausted. Things must have been bad in Haszen if the residents were burning furniture.

My own situation was even more immediately concerning. Had I done the right thing?

Leaving with Thomas had been my plan since I'd met the king that first night, but as soon as he'd put a dagger to my throat, all my plans had seemed foolish and hollow. I'd gone along with anyway, because there hadn't been another option at the time—at least, not one that my mind had come up with immediately. When he'd admitted he'd never loved me, it had sealed my confusion. Was it the fact he'd taken advantage of the situation instead of waiting for me to come up with something that wasn't quite so . . . dangerous?

Or was it just that we'd finally become honest with each other?

It didn't matter. Whatever he'd said, whatever he'd thought about us, I'd been convinced we'd marry one day. He'd never said as much in so many words, but his actions had spoken for him, hadn't they? The kisses, the smiles, the small gifts of eggs and milk he'd left for Mama some days . . . had they been a lie?

I rolled to my side and closed my eyes. There were too many questions to contemplate right then, especially when we'd chosen Haszen as our haven because of the map. It wasn't anywhere near a border, so we were protected from raids. Wildfires? Perhaps, though the amount of snow and water in the creeks made that unlikely. What else had Father Gerritt mentioned?

Illnesses. Earthquakes. Floods. Blizzards that put the entire region at risk.

Not for the first time, I couldn't help but wonder what the purpose of a vague glowing area on a map was. They obviously didn't expect a queen to know, but how could we decide whether to send soldiers or physicians? Perhaps the scout party traveled with an array of skilled men to handle whatever came up.

Warmth settled over me as the heat of the newly stoked fire began to fill the room, and my eyes grew heavy. Moments from drifting off, map or not, I jerked awake at the sound of voices below. A knot in the wood floor? I rolled off of the mattress and found it, smaller than a finger, but any void was enough to let the words of the angry man downstairs fill my ears.

"You should have known better than to bring her here, Thomas."

It was the man who'd sent me upstairs in the first place.

"I couldn't very well leave her in the woods." Thomas's placating tone was something I was intimately familiar with. "Not with the weather this time of year."

"Better the wolves get her than get us."

My cheeks flushed, and not from the fire. He dared to wish for my death when I'd done nothing wrong? I'd acted as a lookout for Thomas on more than one occasion—how could this man question my loyalty like he was?

"Riette's no wolf, that's for certain." Thomas's laughed echoed; I heard it through the knothole and from outside the door. "Just a child trying to find her way in a world she has no control over—though she thinks she does. She'll find out she's just as weak as everyone else in Meirdre, and that unless we prevail, that won't change."

I pulled away from the hole and turned to bury my face in the blanket. Screaming was out of the question, but in all my life, I'd never wanted to shout and cry and stomp and slap someone this badly. This was what he thought of me? Everything else had truly been a lie.

A child.

Weak.

No control.

I leaned back on the mattress and squeezed my eyes shut, then rolled to the floor and put my ear back to the hole.

". . . suppose it won't matter in another few months. Once you let the armies of Vassian in, he'll be dead, and you'll be a hero."

Thomas laughed, but it sounded morose through the ceiling. "Not if I can't get there. King Damir has refused to authorize an invasion unless I personally assure him Laurent is dead, and the people will peacefully exchange his rule for another. He's not interested in a war, nor can he afford one."

I covered a gasp.

"No one will agree to another despot," a third voice replied.

"Doesn't matter." Thomas went quiet for a moment. "After Laurent is gone, they'll believe anything we tell them, no matter how erroneous it is— and it's not as though Damir won't reward us for presenting him his new domain. No more hunger, no more scarcity. Can you imagine?"

"When you put it like that . . ." It was the first man, the one who—probably rightfully, at this point—

hadn't wanted me around. "All right, Thomas. You may proceed. When it's safe, head for Vassian and make your deal with Damir." He chuckled. "But I want to be named in your list of those who receive the earnings."

"Always, Lennert."

I sneezed, then froze.

"Thomas . . . go check for eavesdroppers."

Thomas sighed, and a few seconds later I heard his footsteps on the stairs. Flinging myself over on the mattress, I closed my eyes and concentrated on my rapid heartbeat. Thomas wouldn't touch me to verify I was asleep, would he? The door opened, and I tried to slow my breathing. The fire was still roaring, and I hoped the crackling hid my short, distressed gasps for air.

"Riette?"

I didn't move. Boards creaked as he moved toward me, and a finger hit my temple.

In, out.

Breathe in, out.

Just like he'd come, he'd disappeared.

"No eavesdroppers," I heard through the floor. "She's fast asleep—not used to riding like we did."

"Good. Because if she learns of your plan, it won't take long for the king's inquisitors to pry it out of her—

if she doesn't tell him herself first. You'll have to make sure she dies before that happens."

"You won't need to worry about her. I'll do whatever it takes."

I woke the next morning, stiff from the hours in the saddle and heartsick over Thomas's betrayal of Meirdre—and of me. My feelings for him mattered little at the moment, though, since any indication I was aware of his plot would be the end of my precarious grasp on life. His leader had convinced me of that. Besides, I had more immediate problems.

I needed to find out why the map had led me here.

I located the chamber pot, and then splashed a little icy water from the wash basin on my face, which went a ways into shedding the rest of my fatigue. I'd need all my wits to pretend to be Thomas's jilted but surviving lover, sticking by his side because I was convinced his cause was right and just, although the smells of sausage and eggs from down below made that pretense easier. I crept downstairs, wondering how they'd greet a woman they'd so easily sentenced to death the night before, but to my surprise, only Thomas sat at the long table, a full plate across from him.

"It was a late night," he said, pointing to the food. "The others are still sleeping, so I went ahead and made something for you."

Part of me wondered if he was making up from what I heard last night, but I sat, the rich smell of butter impossible to ignore.

"I appreciate it. After yesterday——" I closed my mouth.

"It was a long day," he said all too calmly, wiping more butter on a piece of brown bread without looking at me. "We both said hurtful things."

"Yes." I speared a piece of sausage with my fork. "But I was wondering . . . if I could borrow the horse. Take a look around town."

"Why?" His gaze was sharp.

"I have to settle somewhere. This looks populated enough; my parents and I might be safe."

Thomas leaned back and folded his arms. "It's too dangerous."

I couldn't argue with someone who was more than willing to kill me to further his own aims. Still, I couldn't get the map out of my head.

"Then I'll go for a walk."

"Rieeeette." It was the same pleading tone I recognized from our childhood, when I'd insisted on climbing trees, and he'd thought it a silly pursuit.

I shoved a roll in my mouth and stood.

I hated having Thomas behind me as we rode through central Haszen. There could be a knife in my kidney before I knew what was happening, but I knew there'd been no leaving the house any other way. He kept his hands to himself though, and I was grateful for that.

The brief snowstorm which had caused us such concern yesterday had blanketed the town in white. The weather had warmed too, and when Thomas said that was usual here this time of year, I realized he hadn't spent all his time in Elternow—more secrets.

Would they ever end? I felt like everything I'd lived so far, everything I'd believe, had been a lie.

"This is where they store what little grain they can." Thomas pointed from behind me.

I made a noncommittal noise. A tour guide wasn't exactly what I'd been after when I'd gone downstairs that morning. He seemed to sense my irritation, for he didn't speak again when we trotted Laurent's expensive horse over the river that separated the town from the sprawl of shacks and cottages to the west. Only a third of them had smoke drifting from their chimneys, and I shivered at what the residents must be feeling. Even on our worst days, Mama and Papa and I had always had wood.

There was no way to know why he'd brought me here. Perhaps he meant to show me this was where my parents and I would be living, once I made my way back to Elternow and convinced them to leave. He was probably right. I stared at the compact houses with a critical eye. There were so many that the king would be hard-pressed to find us.

A few people waved at us as we passed, and I did the same in return, my lips pressed together. Our horse was well-fed; I couldn't help wondering if they were hoping he collapsed in the middle of the road so they could partake. How could Laurent justify feeding these animals when his people went hungry?

I pushed the question to the very far corner of my mind. How could anyone justify half the evil things they did? I'd never know the answer, and searching for it would only drive one mad.

"This isn't so bad," I said over my shoulder. "Lots of places to hide."

"Mmm. I think you'd survive here, yes."

A chin ran down my forearms at his mention of survival, but before I could come up with a reply that didn't let him know what I'd heard last night, the horse stumbled. I grabbed at the reins in Thomas's hands, pulling us to a stop. The horse was too trained to falter, and it only took a moment to realize he hadn't.

The earth was moving.

Thomas seemed to sense the tremors a fraction of a second after I did. He kneed the stallion again, sending us flying down the street toward the empty fields in the east. I didn't argue. The ground rolled and slid underneath us, making anything faster than a trot difficult, but the way the two-story homes swayed on either side of us was a greater concern.

As when we'd galloped out of the castle, I clung to the front of the saddle, my bare fingers numb. Thomas urged our mount on. A scream echoed somewhere behind us, followed by a sound I could only describe as the end of the world.

I looked back, knowing what I'd see. Wood and stone lay in the road where we'd been walking just a minute before. Two homes or three? I couldn't tell through the haze of dust.

"We're almost out of the center of town." Thomas spoke loudly in my ear; the sound of screams and lumber cracking was almost ear-splitting.

I nodded, then froze upon the frightened horse. I'd known this was going to happen. I'd come here because the map had warned me—running away was out of the question. Another shriek cut through the dust, followed by sobs. A woman was dashing down the street, covered in dust, her eyes wide.

There was no time to think. I yanked on the free side of the reins, then slid from the saddle, almost reaching the ground before Thomas's hand clamped down on my arm.

"I have to go help them!"

He yanked me back up by my wrist, and I cried out.

"You'll sit right there. They're vermin, not worth saving."

"Not—" In front of him once again, I twisted backward the best I could, praying I'd misheard. His face, cold and unemotional, told me I wasn't. That woman's expression would haunt me forever, and he was . . . he was ignoring it all, just to save his own skin. "They're people, Thomas!"

"And your pity is slowing us down."

He whistled, loud, and the stallion bolted. Not knowing what else to do, I clawed at him, screaming at him to let me go. I didn't need him. I didn't need the horse. I'd find my way back to Elternow and save Mama and Papa from the king's revenge all on my own.

"Fine."

He called me a name under his breath, then shoved me, hard, and I slid off the saddle. It wasn't the first time I'd fallen from a horse—though it was the first time I'd been *pushed*—and I rolled to the side before clasping my hands over my head. As soon as the hoofbeats grew distant, I looked up.

The earth had stopped rolling, but that was all I could determine. Dust flew through the air, and I coughed as I checked my injuries. There was a scrape on my temple, and I'd landed oddly on my ankle again, but nothing seemed to be broken. I lay there, waiting for the ground to resume pitching, but it stayed still. The deathly silence that had followed the earthquake turned to screams and shouts.

I pushed myself to my feet, ignoring how the dust had turned the light coating of snow into a sticky mess. I could help. This was what I'd been sent here for, and the purpose revitalized me. Picking through the rubble, I made my way toward where I'd last seen the woman. I might not have been a mother, but my heart understood somehow. I could search, I could hold her while she cried, I could—

"Well." A man's voice cut through the panic all around me. I tore my gaze from the commotion down the street. "What have we here?"

I looked up, my body knowing before my mind.

Willem.

I hadn't seen the captain of the Meirdre Royal

Guard since the night I'd met Laurent in the throne room. He had a line of dust down his uniform—even he hadn't escaped the tremor unscathed—but like me, he appeared otherwise uninjured. I stared at the silk of his jacket, unable to reconcile it with the surrounding disaster, unable to force my feet to run.

He grinned at me—or maybe my motionlessness— then pulled my arms behind me, lifting me off the ground. I kicked and screamed then, but none of the people who passed us on the streets paid me any heed. One more distraught woman, hysterical over the loss of her home and possibly her children—why would they care?

"You can keep fighting," he snarled in my ear, "but it won't change a thing."

He shoved me around a corner, toward a waiting cart with tall sides and no roof. I'd expected soldiers, but there were none, and I flailed, my confusion slowing my reflexes. But that also meant there was a chance I could talk myself out of this mess. I couldn't escape from a squad of men, but I maybe could convince Willem to let me go.

"Captain." My breath was short, from the dust that still hung around us and my own fear. "You don't understand. You have to listen. They need assistance. Medical help. I can save people, if you'd only let me—"

"I understand well enough. You brought him a dagger, then escaped with him. You thought you'd get away with that?"

I hadn't brought Thomas the dagger—there was no doubt he'd picked it from a careless guard—but Willem would never believe my pleas. With a firm hand on my arms, he pushed me into the cart and shoved me to the floor. I landed on my side with a grunt and examined my routes of escape. The wood was already cold under my hip, and it would only get worse as we began our trek back to the castle and frigid air began to flow around and under me.

"You had so much," Willem said, yanking chains from a pile in the corner. "And you threw it all away. And for what?"

"I—"

I slammed my mouth shut at his accuracy. Or maybe it was the weight of the chains he'd secured around my wrist and ankles. They hung heavy about my joints, and even before he fastened an iron collar to the opposite end to a catch on the top of the wagon, I realized there would be no escape.

"Quiet." He pulled a sack over my head, and darkness joined my silence. "You can tell the inquisitors."

CHAPTER TWELVE

I KNELT ON THE STONE FLOOR, WAVERING FROM SIDE TO side in fear. The iron around my wrists and ankles had rubbed my skin raw during our trip, and my muddy dress did nothing to shield me from the cold of the throne room. Blind though I'd been on the trip, I'd still been able to tell that it had been snowing so hard that drifts formed in the open wagon around me, and I'd be lucky if I kept all my toes.

Not that keeping them would matter for much longer. Frostbite or no frostbite, they'd march me to the execution chamber all the same. Not until the snow ended, naturally, since Meirdrean executions always took place on a clear night—legend had it that there was a tunnel in the ceiling of the death chamber, a hole in the layers of rock above the dungeon that allowed the condemned to see the stars one last time. Such were the whispers, but I was going to learn the truth. It might have been snowing when they'd brought me back, but this time of the year the storms would be waning, which meant my remaining days were few. Willem had reminded me of my fate when he'd hauled me out of the wagon upon our return, and I had no reason to doubt him.

It would be Thomas's fate, too.

For after Willem had found me, my heart hadn't had the chance to stop pounding before Thomas had been shoved into the cart as well—and judging by his sporadic unconsciousness, he might have fought harder than I had. Not that I'd been all that surprised at his capture. I wanted to look at him, kneeling next to me, but I could only focus on Laurent's boots as he rose from his throne and walked down the stairs.

"I suppose there's no accounting for taste." His tone was smooth, unbothered, almost bored. "Though I admit I'm surprised you chose him over me."

I looked up then, but he turned his attention to Thomas before I could plead for my life—or tell him that I'd chosen no one.

"Thomas Wennink," he said, "Do you have anything to say for yourself?"

Thomas swore at him, but the words were so

slurred I couldn't understand them, which was probably for the best. He'd barely closed his mouth when the hilt of a sword in his abdomen silenced him once more, and Laurent's boots turned back toward me.

"And you?"

I wasn't stupid. Even in the midst of my desperate fear and frantic desire to beg for leniency, I'd known, as every Meirdrean subject did, that anything I could say would be grounds for capricious and arbitrary torture before the imposition of my sentence. I swallowed my fear, along with the last of my hope.

"Nothing? I think I deserve an explanation of why my betrothed rode off with a known rebel. Someone"—his voice rose to a shout—"who would see me dead!"

I jerked upright, and though I'd wanted to hide my fear, I could feel it on my face. I could sense it, and for some reason I wanted Laurent to see me as courageous.

"Will—will my explanation change anything?" I asked quietly.

He stared at me, and for a fleeting moment I saw the man who'd asked if I could ever love him. The one who'd wanted a marriage—a genuine one. Would I live after all? I took two quick breaths, savoring the hope that had filled my heart, then his expression turned as hard as the sword at his side.

"No," he replied slowly, shattering my courage. "It will not."

I lowered my head.

"You have both," he went on, "been found guilty of high treason. Therefore, as is my duty as the King of Meirdre, I sentence you, Thomas Wennink and Riette Kaleveld, to death—as soon as the snow ceases."

Light glinted against the stone outside as I tried to wedge a fingernail into the shackles once more. Footsteps approached, and the lock clicked, but I was beyond caring if the visitor saw what I was doing. I didn't look up. Whether I was bound for the torture room or the hangman or managed to free myself by my own efforts, I'd be free soon, though I'd never be able to rescue Thomas now. I could hear him somewhere in the distance, his screams alternating with moans, and for some reason I felt pity for him, even after what he'd done to me and tried to do to Meirdre. For a long while I'd sat with my hands over my ears, but that hadn't been nearly enough to drown out his sounds of agony.

"Riette, stop."

I yanked my bleeding fingers from the shackles and looked up at Father Gerritt. He settled down next to me, apparently not caring that his robes had already become soaked with mud and the melted snow I'd dragged in. The white execution gown I wore couldn't look much better, but I'd been beyond caring what I looked like as soon as Hek had handed it to me.

"I have to get out of here," I said.

Thomas's earlier screams stopped, filling the cell with silence, and Father Gerritt didn't answer as he unpacked the small bag at his waist. I'd hoped for a key to the shackles or maybe a dagger, but as near as I could tell in the shadows of my cell, it was only a bottle of oil. I could do nothing but stare at his hands, spotted and wrinkled, as he prayed over it. Mine would never look like that, for I would never grow old enough for them to age. This was it. There was no escape, and even he knew it.

"Father—"

"In a moment—let me do this first. He said he wouldn't interfere."

His firmness silenced me. Was he so concerned they'd come for me before he finished his ritual? Even the king knew better than to interfere in the administration of last rites—he'd never cross a priest, would never be responsible for the damnation of my soul, I supposed.

I wanted to laugh at the hypocrisy.

Cinnamon and myrrh overtook the stench of sweat and urine as he swiped the oil on my forehead, and some of my terror turned to anger. What did he think this would accomplish? That it would save me? Heal me in advance from the mortal injuries they meant to impart on my body? If the past few weeks had taught me anything, it was that life didn't happen like that.

His palm settled on the top of my head, and I fought the urge to scream at him.

"Receive her into Your merciful arms and permit her to walk in Your light forevermore," he murmured. "There. I would be remiss in my duties if I didn't take care of that first. You have something you wish to confess?"

"Confess?" My voice cracked, and I shook my head. He was so close to finding out the truth, and though I'd been ready to tell anyone, now that I was standing on the brink, it was impossible. I would take the secret of Thomas's treachery to my grave. "Father, I've done nothing wrong."

"We've all done something," he pointed out. "Even me, believe it or not."

The cackle that sprang from my throat was perhaps inappropriate, but what did it matter anymore?

"I doubt you know anything about sin," I replied with no small amount of spite.

"It's funny you use those words. Doubt. Sin." He eyed me with more than casual interest. "Doubt can be a sin, you know."

My religious education had been sparse enough that I only had the vaguest idea of what he was talking about. I made a noise of assent anyway. If he believed this was his final chance to save my soul, I'd let him try. It couldn't hurt.

"Then we're in agreement on that? Good—though I don't think you suffer from that particular malady."

My eyes grew hot. As it wasn't bad enough to be waiting on my certain death, he was confusing me, and my confusion only added to the humiliation. I wasn't unintelligent, but I wasn't educated either, and his reminder that I lacked something most others in the castle possessed fell harshly upon me.

"Father, I don't know what you're trying to get at."

"Well, let's start with your theft of the horse."

"I didn't steal anyone's horse. Thomas did. If I'd tried to change his mind—"

For the first time since I'd entered the dungeon with the berries, I realized any escape might not have ended the way I'd have hoped. Thomas didn't love me. He'd used me. Would he have truly cut my throat if I'd fought against his plan? Likely he would have. He'd told Lennert he'd kill me if I made my way back to the castle and told anyone of his plans for Meirdre. Yes, he'd have doubtless killed me if I'd tried to escape. More heat joined the tears, only this time, it warmed me to my core with fear and rage. I'd trusted someone who would have sacrificed me for his cause.

"Father—I do have something to tell you." The story tumbled out. Vassian, King Damir, how Thomas planned to use them to overthrow Laurent, only to leave our kingdom in the same poverty as before— perhaps worse. "I tried to tell Willem, and he didn't listen, so now . . . I don't see any way around this. We're both going to die."

"There." He reached out a hand to my upper arm. "That wasn't so hard, was it?"

It hadn't been, but my confusion didn't abate.

"But I didn't confess to anything."

"You just confessed to trusting the wrong person. Not that you did anything wrong in doing so, but I suspect you needed to acknowledge it yourself. For your own peace of mind, you understand. No one should go to eternity holding a secret like that. You can't forgive him if you can't accept what he did to you and planned to do to Meirdre."

I drew my knees to my chest, the shackles clanging against the chain which held me to the wall, then laid my head down on them.

"I was so stupid," I whispered. "So naïve."

"We all have our moments," he replied easily. "Now, the treason."

I didn't answer. There was no point. Depending on what else I said, they could still torture me, and why would I subject myself to pain like that?

"I do not think," he began, "that we have time to address whether the general crime of treason itself is a sin, though I have my own opinions, of course. In a thousand years, men much more learned than I haven't been able to agree." He leaned back against the wall and folded his arms, a casual gesture I didn't particularly care for at that moment. "Your individual treason, on the other hand . . ."

"Spare me," I spat at him from my hunched position, my throat half closed. "If you'd experienced half of what I did as a child—"

"Who says I didn't? I rather think you're not familiar with my entire history."

I shut my mouth, and he went on.

"I was born in Saalben—yes, that Saalben you know as one of the poorest villages in the realm. My mother was practically a child herself, unmarried and young. They took me from her and left me on the steps of the local church one winter night, hoping I'd die— but that they could assuage themselves of any guilt by making certain I passed as physically close to the Lord as possible."

He cleared his throat. "Only I didn't. I spent my first years in an orphanage. If we had little food, discipline wasn't in short supply. I'll spare you the remainder of the details, but I learned to hate King Julian, and later, his son Laurent."

"You don't seem like you hate him now."

"Saying otherwise would shorten my life, would it not?" He gave me a slight smile. "None of us are wholly sinless or wholly evil, and I do what I can to make sure the balance of his heart and works are tipped toward good. It's never-ending work, believe me."

"I can imagine." I didn't hide my bitterness.

"And it's drudgery we all share a responsibility for."

He was probably becoming tired of my hateful laughter, but I couldn't stop myself.

"You can't possibly believe I have any responsibility for that man's evil deeds, nor the power to persuade him to act otherwise."

"Maybe. Maybe not. I'm no seer. I can't predict the future, and I can't hazard to guess what may or may not have happened had you chosen to go forward with a marriage you consented to. I do know you were chosen for one reason or another, and that you decided to throw that summons away. That's the treason I speak of. Not against the king, but against Someone infinitely more powerful and merciful."

How could he speak of God now? "Thomas and I are both going to die now, Father. There's no way around it."

"There is." He sounded too confident. "And I think you know what you need to do to save yourself."

"I won't do it. I don't care what happens to me in this life or the next." His figure disappeared into a blur of dark tears. "I helped save Meirdre from Vassian by telling you what I did, but I won't help Laurent oppress my own people. I won't wish for his death, but I also won't help protect him. Someone else can take up that obligation, because I refuse."

"Oh, child." The disappointment flowed from him, landing heavily on my shoulders. "You think this gift that's been bestowed upon you was meant to protect *him?*"

CHAPTER THIRTEEN

THERE WASN'T MUCH ONE COULD DO IN A DUNGEON cell on their last day of life but cry and pray, and as much as I'd sworn to be brave when the time ultimately came, it was a foolish optimism. Some could walk to the chamber without sobbing and with their head held high, but I, it turned out, was not one of them. By the time the king swept in, two guards at his side, I was limp with exhaustion and dehydration. The floor beneath my cheek was soaked with my tears, and when I lifted my head at their entrance, a puddle remained, proof of my cowardice.

So much for valor.

The king looked down at me, his lip twisted in disgust. "Pleading and weeping for mercy is a waste of breath." He gestured at the guards. "They'll drag you out if they must, but I would hope you have enough honor to walk yourself."

Even if I'd wanted to, I was too numb to plead. And I didn't as they removed the shackles, or as I stood and crept forward to where the ceiling allowed my full height. But when they fastened my hands before me with a rough cord, the tears returned. They didn't stop when one of the men slipped the noose around my neck, scratching my skin, and I closed my eyes in fear. He tossed the free end to the ground, and I fought for air, though I was almost certain my inability to breathe was panic, and nothing more.

They weren't done with me yet.

I was certain of that when they pulled me into the corridor and my eyes adjusted once more. Thomas was there, surrounded by guards, likewise restrained, though livid bruises showed on his exposed skin. We were both pushed forward without ceremony, and somehow my legs kept moving.

Stone.

Mud.

Melted snow.

Stone.

I stared at them alternating under my bare feet, watched the hem of my gown grow dark as the rope trailed along behind me. Thomas's moans sounded in my left ear, in my right, the quiet prayers of Father Gerritt. No one else spoke, and even though I wanted to scream, something kept me quiet. Fear? Acceptance? I'd come so far from the girl who'd promised to save Thomas or else.

Still, watching him die and then hanging myself was better than what Father Gerritt had suggested. I knew, behind the traditional prayers, that he was asking for me to change my mind, but there was no chance of that. I'd made my decision.

My guards pulled me to a halt and bound my knees with a rope. I forced myself to look up as they did, at the gallows in the center of the chamber, a hole over it. No snow fell to the floor, no rain dripped from the opening. There might have been stars somewhere up there, but I wouldn't know for certain until they stood me underneath. Even so, I could see them in my mind, brilliant and dazzling, like someone had flung a handful of diamonds into the heavens. A vast and eerie darkness stretched between them, incandescent with unthinkably distant stars.

While two others pushed Thomas underneath the scaffolding, I blinked away the vision of the heavens. He stumbled then, whether out of fear or pain I couldn't tell. His rope was flung over top, and I closed my eyes, unable to watch the rest. Forcing me to watch

Thomas's execution before my own, I'd finally realized, was another part of my sentence, one I would not willingly participate in. But my lack of vision made me unsteady, even with them holding on to my arms, and I opened my eyes almost immediately.

The executioner began to speak. "Thomas Wennink, having committed treason, your life is forfeit unless the king, in all his mercy, wishes to grant you clemency."

There was a pause, a heavy silence in the stone chamber, but his suggestion was a formality. The king rarely—if ever—witnessed executions, and his presence at my side wouldn't change the outcome.

"Then may you be forgiven of your crimes and be returned to the arms of the—"

"Stop!"

My heart thudded at Thomas's scream; I grew light-headed, even in the chill of winter that drifted through the hole. So dizzy I sagged against the wall, against the guards who'd grabbed me. It didn't make sense, and that was the only thing I could repeat in my mind as my surroundings blurred. I might not have courage, but he did, more than anyone I'd ever known. He wouldn't have begged them to stop. He wouldn't have humiliated himself like that.

And then I realized, as I was jerked back to my feet

and the chamber sharpened about me again, that the scream had been mine.

King Laurent waved his hand at the executioner and turned to face me with a new and frightening interest. It was that curiosity that kept me upright, even though I had no faith that I had stopped anything for long. In giving me the attention I'd screamed for, he was merely toying with me, like a cat might with an injured bird.

"Stop?" he asked, so close I could see the blood pulsing in a vein in his neck, could smell that he'd had a glass of wine with supper. "You order me to stop, standing here bound and half strangled? Just who do you think you are?"

I wanted to duck my head away, but the heavy rope prevented much movement. Fine, then. If that's what it took to impart me with artificial bravery, I would take it, however reluctantly.

"I have a deal to make with you," I said. Swallowing was difficult with the rope pressing on my throat; saliva welled up in my mouth. "Here. Now."

"A deal?" he scoffed. "A peasant girl whose life is forfeit has nothing to offer me."

I did, though. I did. But which was worse? Falling into eternity with the knowledge I'd failed my kingdom—or making the decision to save it, knowing

I'd be forever bound to a man who'd once wanted me dead?

"You said I could save a prisoner by marrying you." I gasped the words. "I will still do so."

He laughed. "You're more foolish than I thought. You think I would marry you now?"

I couldn't breathe any longer and shrank back against the wall, sending a violent shiver down my spine. "Take this off my neck and I'll tell you."

"No." The answer was immediate, but his curious gaze didn't falter.

"You can always," I whispered, "hang me when I'm done talking."

"You demand too much." He gave the guard a sharp order, anyway. The man wasn't gentle about removing the noose, and he'd probably left splinters of rope in my skin, but I didn't care. Thomas, I noticed over the king's shoulder, was watching with his mouth open, the rope still tossed over the top of the beam.

"Riette, you can't do this!" he shouted. "Not for me. There will be others. Don't give that man—"

"It's not only for you," I interrupted before the guards could hit him again. I wanted to tell him so much more, but now wasn't the time. I doubted it would ever be the time, so I focused on the king again. "You don't want him hearing this. Or the guards."

He narrowed his eyes and tilted his head before ordering the guards and executioner out. They dragged Thomas with them, and as the chamber emptied, leaving me alone there with Laurent, I suddenly thought better of my abrupt bravery.

"So?" he asked, when I didn't speak. "You had something to tell me?"

"I'm a—I'm a crownkeeper." I looked past him, at the stone wall on the far side of the chamber. "The one you've been waiting on, the one you never actually believed you'd choose out of all the girls in Meirdre, the one our people need. Kill me if you must, but you'll regret it. Maybe one lonely night while you're staring at the ceiling wondering what you could have done better for your people. Or maybe only when you have to tell your advisors that you murdered the one person who could have given forewarning that your borders have been breached."

"You're no crownkeeper." His smile grew. "You're not only a traitor but a liar. That power is gifted only to queens. Connected to Creation you might be, but without our marriage, you're nothing but a might-have-been. And since the law forbids divorce or the execution of a royal wife, I certainly won't take a chance on marrying a charlatan now."

"Juliana and I—" My chest was so tight that I

might as well have been immured, stealing my last oxygen all on my own. "We were in the chapel. She thought it would be amusing to see what I looked like with—she put the crown on my head. And ever since, I see the cracks in the borders. I see raiding parties assembling. The earthquake in Haszen. That map on the floor of the ballroom—it shows me everything."

"Who told you about the map?" I didn't answer, and he stepped even closer and shouted in my ear. "Who told you?"

"No one told me. You know what a closely held secret it is, just like I do now. Juliana led me through the ballroom right after we visited the chapel, and it was lit like diamonds, right at the border with Nantoise. I didn't even know what I was seeing. It confused me, and then it terrified me, and now . . . it calls to me."

I hadn't even realized until now. Maybe it was the magic, but I rather believed it was my own stubbornness. But that was gone now, leaving me empty—and only one thing could fill that void.

"I don't believe you."

"But you can test me," I answered quietly. "If the map is lit, send scouts. You can verify what I'm saying is true."

"And if it's not lit?"

My head fell to my chest. I didn't answer. I knew

what his response would be.

He hollered for one of the guards. To me, he added, "You have one chance. If the map isn't lit, or if I found out that you're lying about this power, I'll make you wish you died today."

My weak legs made it difficult to climbs up the stairs, even with guards on each elbow. Thomas had been returned to the gallows, insurance against any thoughts I might have of escape. One shout from my companions would end his life, so I walked quietly next to them, through empty stone corridors and the occasional storage chamber.

The servants were gone. *Celebrating the eve of the feast,* the king said as we walked, as though he was introducing me to court life and not putting me to a test that could end my own. I scarcely heard his words, could hardly see anything in the fog that hung around me. The men pulled me to a stop, and I looked up, confused, only to see myself standing in the center of the ballroom.

"Look around your kingdom." With no small amount of mocking, Laurent threw his hands in the air and spun in a circle. "See anything?"

I wanted to rub my eyes, but the guards had a vise grip on my arms. I blinked, the dizziness and nausea almost unbearable. They spun me, slowly, after I kicked my feet out the side in a silent order to let me turn, and I stared.

And stared.

And stared.

At Meirdre.

At Vassian.

At the Kalcine River.

At Elternow and Haszen and the Arsele Forest.

There was nothing. The map was as quiet and still as the stones that made up the dungeon where I would now die. My eyes, filled with fear, met Father Gerritt's, and he shook his head. It was odd, but I felt like I'd let him down more than anything else. Would he continue to pray for me as they walked me back to that chamber? Or had even he given up hope?

"She doesn't see anything. Hang him. Immediately." Laurent made a disgusted noise, then stroked a few fingers under my chin. "And take her back down and prepare her for her own execution."

He hadn't pressed on my throat, but the ballroom began to spin. It'd done that the first time I'd seen the map glow, but this time it was panic and nothing more. He was going to take me away from the map, and right now staying with it was the thing I wanted most. More than saving Thomas. More than hurting Laurent.

"No. Stop."

My voice broke as I yanked myself away from the guards. They didn't catch me quickly enough, and I fell to my knees, tears dampening the marble. They'd have to lift me up, carry me back to the dungeon, and I didn't care who heard my cries. Let Laurent cleanse the mess he'd created.

"Get her up."

A deep pain shot through my elbow as one of them yanked on my wrist. My feet slid on the polished floor, and I tried to claw at the wood with my free hand. Anything to buy myself more time. The guards dropped me, and I grunted as I hit the ground, blinking furiously. There was something—

"Stop!" The entire wing had probably heard my scream. "You have to stop. It's there. It's right there."

"What?" Laurent's shadow hovered me. "What's right there? You see something?"

Tears streaming down my face—from relief now, not fear—I pointed at the shimmering piece of wood not a foot from where I knelt, though I knew no one else could see what I saw.

"Harnow. Something's happening at Harnow."

CHAPTER FOURTEEN

I HADN'T SPOKEN SINCE THE KING AND HIS MEN HAD ridden off. Not to Hek, not even to Father Gerritt, who'd stayed in this dank cell with me for the past two days, promising me it was no worse than the vigils he'd kept in the past. I hadn't replied to that argument, and eventually, he'd given up trying to force me to speak and had resorted to praying over me—when he wasn't making me drink what little water I'd been allowed. I did that, grudgingly. It was the only thing keeping me sane, especially I hadn't slept at all, too consumed with the threat Laurent had left me with.

If you're lying, I'll make you regret it.

I believed him. I believed he was angry and frightened and was capable of almost anything.

Father Gerritt finished his latest prayer and shifted

closer to me, taking my left hand in his. He'd extracted a promise from me—a nod, at least—that I wouldn't try to unfasten the shackles, but he must have known I'd break it. My prior attempts had left my fingers bloody and swollen, and he shook his head as he washed them again with a rag and a little water.

"You're going to die of an infection if you don't stop this," he said.

The calm prediction almost made me scream.

Almost.

I jerked my hand away and fell to my side in a silent command that he stop his suggestions, the chains rattling as I did. What did it matter if I died of an infection? Would it be more painful than the noose? I doubted it, though it wouldn't matter in the end. In any case, death was so near that I was more in need of his prayers for my soul than his medical care.

He scooted back into his corner. Maybe Father Gerritt had seen something in my hands that I hadn't. I was finally warm, after all, and down here that meant one thing: a fever. Then—the jingle of keys sounded outside. No, the noise had to be a hallucination.

But the door was hauled open, and in the light of the lamp outside, I saw a single shadow. Not Hek, since he'd never appeared without a guard, and I still had what he considered adequate water. Likely not the executioner, not here on his own. I wanted to claw at the collar in one last effort to free myself from the chains which held me to the wall, but I held my breath and clawed at my palms instead. The hours of thirst and pain and fear made it too burdensome for me to speculate further.

"It was just a few cases," the figure said as he entered and sat the oil lamp on the floor. "Just a few cases."

He limped, as if days in the saddle had been unkind to him, and straightened even more sluggishly. The words were listless. Not drunk, but exhausted, like the speaker had used all his energy on what he'd seen. He stopped just short of where I huddled, hands on his hips. He might not have been able to see me, but I had grown used to the gloom of the dungeon, and I could see him.

Laurent.

"Measles, in several young children," he went on, as if to himself. "It was beginning to spread."

I told you so was less than helpful. Instead, I pressed my lips together and waited for whatever came next. I recognized his expression—the realization had dawned on him as he'd ridden back to the castle. He knew I was telling the truth, and he was furious and resigned and hopeful all at once. I'd given him a way to protect his power, and I could only pray he reached for it.

"The villagers quarantined themselves two weeks ago. Not even a scout in or out. There's no way you could have known," he said to himself as much as to me. "Unless you saw it in the map."

"I wasn't lying." My mouth had become so dry I could barely speak. The way he was looking at me was just like I used to look at the slivers of dried beef Mama would pull from some dark corner of the cellar after a long winter—I'd hated them, even though it wasn't their fault they were the only meat left. "I will not swear much to you, but I swear that."

"I still don't need to marry you," he replied with a glance at the chains. I didn't like the contemplation I saw in that glance. "I could just as easily keep you down here. Build a duplicate of the map in stone. You'd have no choice but to watch it for me."

We both knew it was a lie—I could see it in his eyes. Not lust, not exactly. Lonely desperation for the wife he'd lost even before securing her. He wouldn't get that love and companionship from me, but if he thought he would? Maybe that would be enough.

"Or what? You'd have me tortured?" I bit off the words, regretting them as soon as they tumbled out. They hadn't done it so far, and I wasn't sure I could survive it. Putting the idea in his head was dangerous, no matter what he thought he felt about me.

"It doesn't matter," Father Gerritt broke in. "She needs contact with the land in order for this to work. The sky, the ground, the snow, the mountains. And she needs the original map, not some poor reproduction created so you can abuse the crownkeeper sent to you. Don't tell me you don't have a clue how the magic works, sire. She's willing to honor your original agreement in order to prevent harm to this kingdom, and I know you want the same, if only to preserve your power. If you allow harm to come to Meirdre—and you would be doing so if you murder her—I doubt your position would remain secure for much longer."

Laurent's sword clattered at his side as he spun around toward him. "You knew about this, didn't you?"

"It was not my secret to tell." He shrugged. "You've been given a glorious gift, sire. The first crownkeeper to appear in over a hundred and fifty years, if I'm not mistaken. I suggest you not squander this gift out of some misguided yearning for revenge."

"And I suggest you keep your nose out of business that doesn't concern you, Father."

The king turned back to me, his expression hard, but we all knew the power in the kingdom had shifted. I could practically see the futures playing out in his mind

—did he grant me mercy, solidifying his hold on Meirdre, or did he let his need for vengeance get the best of him and force me under the gallows, ridding himself of my ability for the rest of his reign?

"And as long as we're being honest, there's something else you need to know," I added. "Thomas, he—he planned to hand Meirdre over to Vassian. He'd made an agreement with King Damir." I quickly related what I'd heard through the knothole at the house in Haszen, watched Laurent's cheeks grow red in fury—and no small amount of fear, I suspected. "I hadn't known what he'd planned. I didn't realize he'd sacrifice Meirdre to elevate his own status. That's not something I can support. It's not something I can allow to happen. I tried to tell Willem, and he—"

"And you want me to free this man."

I shook my head. Naïve I might have been at one point, but even I knew Thomas would never leave this dungeon alive.

"I know he can never be freed." My voice cracked for the last time. The words were so heavy. So final.

"No." His immediate agreement made my stomach turn. "He cannot."

The cell fell quiet. I had saved my life—probably. But I hadn't saved Thomas, and that was why I was down here in the first place.

"But he can live," I replied.

"No," he repeated. "He cannot."

"He's not a threat to you while he's imprisoned. As long as he can't meet with King Damir, there's no risk to you, no threat to Meirdre."

"Has your captivity addled you, my dear? That's not the tradition, and outside of that, I have no reason to allow it. He's to be freed or executed, as was his sentence prior to your arrival. And he will not be freed." With that decree, he turned back toward the open door, snapping his fingers at a guard outside. "Bring him to the chamber at once."

"It's the arrangement King Arend made in his original surrender agreement with the duke," I called after him without thinking. "I'd argue it's more of a tradition than the one you celebrate now."

Laurent turned, a strange sort of delight in his expression. "You remember the story."

"I do," I said, frowning at his expression. He was pleased I'd remembered?

He paused, backlit there in the doorway. "And if I agree to save his life, you agree to marry me? You will live at Lochfeld, will watch the map for me, will protect Meirdre until you die?"

I nodded. He hadn't mentioned loving him, and I could easily agree to everything he *had* asked for.

He crouched before me and ran a shaking finger down my jawbone. "Why would you do this?" he asked. "You don't love me, and you don't love that man. You have no reason to save either one of us. Are you that afraid of death?"

Telling him how I felt called to protect Meirdre was too intimate. He hadn't earned that trust and likely never would—nor did I particularly feel like vocalizing it to myself. Acting on it was one thing. Admitting it was something altogether different and frightening.

"Yes." The lie slid through my lips. "I am."

An oppressive quiet fell heavy on me as he watched my breathing slow. I couldn't tell what he was thinking. Of all the powers I could have been gifted, why couldn't mind-reading have been one of them?

"There will be no formal ceremony," he said at long last, standing suddenly, as if to make the difference in our circumstances clear one last time. "As a reminder of what you've done, you will marry me as befits a traitor—in that gown you're wearing now. Here. Down below."

Hope. I felt it for the first time, and when I glanced at Father Gerritt, his head, lowered in relief, only served to confirm my optimism. The king's words sounded like a threat, something demeaning, and maybe they were partly that—but they were also so much more.

He had made his decision. I would live. So would Thomas.

I knew, because he was negotiating with me now. Not with a peasant, not with a prisoner, but with an equal, as he had the first night I'd come here. His desire for equilibrium was his strength, though I'm sure he'd consider it a weakness if he stopped to think about.

"I don't care what I wear," I replied. I wanted to stand, to equalize us even more, but the clanking of chains would defeat the purpose, so I remained still.

"No?" His brows rose. "You will never hold the title of queen while I am alive. I'll find some lessor title to satisfy most of the gossip. Still, the court will wonder why, and I will forbid you from explaining."

"Let them wonder." He certainly didn't know much about me if he thought I cared. "I only ask that my parents do not suffer on my account."

"Our original agreement regarding them stands," he said without hesitation. "You needn't worry about your parents."

My shoulders sank even further in relief.

He grinned, and for the first time I worried he had the upper hand somehow. One-sided negotiation it was to be, then. No matter. He knew what I had to offer and what I could take away. Any threats and propositions from his side would be laughable.

"Thomas Wennink was sentenced to be whipped before his execution. A hundred lashes. I commute his sentence, if you take his place as punishment for your treason. Agree to *that*, dear Riette, and you have your bargain."

My pulse quickened, and a foul sensation overcame my stomach. I hadn't noticed the whip in the executioner's hand that day, so distraught had I been by the gallows, and the sickening truth hit me like a bolt of lightning. They hadn't intended to make Thomas's death easy. They'd planned to whip him as he stood under the noose, knowing once he could no longer remain on his feet—much sooner than a hundred lashes—he'd slowly strangle all on his own. The entire performance was more macabre than I'd ever imagined.

"Ah." His grin fell, an odd gravity taking its place. "Not so easy to agree to my conditions now, is it? You shouldn't have shown your hand so early, my dear."

I turned my face into the shadows so he couldn't see the tears running down my cheeks. A hundred lashes would kill me. It was enough to leave a powerful man half dead—though it wasn't as if they cared what happened to someone who already had his head in a noose. Did I care enough for Meirdre—for Thomas—to allow him to do this? I'd made my peace with marrying a man I didn't love in order to save the kingdom, but no one had ever told me the sacrifice would be physically painful as well.

The king knelt again and turned my head to face him once more. "So? The executioner is in the chamber waiting for your decision. Who will it be? Both of you, to the death . . . or just you, until you beg me for mercy?"

"Ten," I whispered, not caring that I'd truly failed at bargaining with him. "Ten lashes, and I'll agree to your conditions."

"Ten? I couldn't possibly absolve you after such trivial suffering. Whatever would you learn from such a lenient sentence?" He wiped my left cheek dry with a tenderness that felt out of place. "Fifteen."

Relieved, I swallowed. He was trying to save face, not harm me—not seriously, at least. I could work with that.

"Twelve," I replied. "In private."

"Do you think I'd have my future wife whipped in front of the court? Only the ones here will ever know of your crimes—that's not a factor you can bargain with. It'll happen right here, this very hour. Thirteen."

He was simply being cruel now, and I knew we'd

reached an impasse. Most of me wanted to tell him to go to hell, that he needed me more than I needed him, but the smallest whisper in the back of my mind was afraid he was holding something over me. I couldn't imagine what that could be, but every negotiation came to an end, didn't it? Most of the time both lost something, but sometimes . . . sometimes only one did.

But none of that mattered.

I could protect Meirdre.

I was destined to protect her.

My heart thumped once, and I spoke before I lost my nerve.

"Thirteen."

CHAPTER FIFTEEN

The evening was warm for late winter, and I was grateful for it as I watched out the open window wearing nothing but a thin chemise. Goosebumps dotted my arms, even in the mild weather, but I had cried out in pain when Juliana tried to dress me properly, so nothing but the chemise it was—and would be for a few days. At least it was silk, and I'd embroidered snowdrops along the hem that reminded me of spring on the moors. It was something, at least. The exquisite stays and gowns? Those would have to be abandoned for at least a month while I healed, something which grated on my new husband.

If I'd only known you would have to dress like a servant for so long, I'd have told the executioner to go easier on you.

He'd told me so as I lay on my stomach on the floor

of the dungeon, sobbing from my wounds. A surprising emotion had welled up at his statement, and I'd tried to swallow my reaction before I could anger him even more. The pain had dulled my focus though, along with all my common sense, and my tears had turned to laughter just long enough for him to stomp out in disgust. The willow bark he'd gone to procure for me had taken away enough of the pain that I eventually stood—with his assistance—and then, with Father Gerritt as a witness, I promised to love and obey someone I hated.

I had to admit he'd come up with a foolproof story. The official account was that I'd been too distraught over my treatment at the hands of my abductor to participate in a formal wedding ceremony. Hek, the executioner, and Willem's royal guard had been silenced by threats of their own demises, and Laurent had carried me up from the dungeon himself, allegedly after I'd identified my captor who'd immediately been hung for his offenses.

Before he'd done that, however, he'd shown me Thomas's new abode—a hole scarcely large enough for him to stand or lie down. I'd leaned against him, too frail to stand on my own. I heard chains, and the drip of water, and the occasional moan, but I hadn't been able to see inside, and that was for the best. I still wasn't sure if the stopover was meant to be a threat or reassurance, and I chose to see it as the latter. It was the only way to quell my fear, to convince myself I'd made the right decision.

Juliana hadn't questioned the story. She'd embraced me with the caution my injuries demanded, then ministered to me as best she could, all the while cursing the man who'd harmed me so. Sara hadn't asked questions either, and I doubted any of the rest of the servants would ever mention the situation again. Not in front of me, at least. For once, rumors and gossip worked in my favor.

"Are you done watching the moon rise?" the king asked from his position by the door.

"Yes." I eyed him warily. It had been an excuse, but I needed time to accept what I'd done.

"Then come to bed, my beloved wife. We have a wedding night to enjoy."

The sneering wasn't going to end anytime soon, then. That was fine—vows or no vows, I didn't feel any particular marital feelings toward him, either. Moving as quickly as my injuries allowed, I perched on the edge of the bed and stared at my hands, clasped in my lap.

The king sank down beside me, and I held my breath, anticipating his touch. Juliana had said it could be pleasurable, but she loved her husband. She'd never imagined intimacy with someone she hated, nor not being able to lie down properly. I'd begged her for more instruction, but she'd demurred, likely having no further suggestions for my battered body.

One palm cupped my cheek, and I closed my eyes as the other settled behind my neck. The caress was gentle—might have been arousing on any other day, even from him—but I arched my back in dread of the moment his touch would reach it. That involuntary motion hurt more than his hands on me, and I cried out as my skin pulled across the fresh wounds.

He frowned, then removed his hands and placed them in his lap. We sat there in silence, next to each other but miles apart, as the moon rose higher out the window, casting a glow on his face and strange shadows in the corners. I couldn't tell what he was thinking. Learning to hide his emotions must have been one of the first things he'd been taught as a child.

But if he was sitting there expressionless, I knew exactly what was running through my mind—how he'd asked me the night of our betrothal ball if I could ever love him. After I'd knelt on the icy stones before the whipping block, after he'd watched without compassion as I screamed in the chains which held me immobile, I suspected he knew the answer to his question then. No willow bark, no soothing bandages, no kind words could ever make up for what he'd done, would ever change my feelings for him.

"Beautiful as you are, I won't take what you're not willing to give without reservation," he said at long last. "And I won't be responsible for causing you further pain. So if I might make a suggestion, it's that we both go to sleep. When you feel differently, you may ask for an audience and inform me."

His pretentiousness almost made me laugh once more, but before I could, my words caught at the obvious guilt in his voice. He didn't deserve to feel guilty about what he'd done to me, but I couldn't very well tell him that, so I only nodded.

"I think that's a fine idea, sire."

He nodded once in return, then scooted to the far side of the bed, burying himself in layers of velvet and wool. After a moment I swung my legs up and joined him, for no other reason but to warm myself. He flinched but didn't pull away as I crept up to him on my side. If I was to share a bed with him tonight to make the servants believe nothing was amiss between us, I was going to get something practical out of it. Warmth was enough.

I stopped before I touched him. Even though his feelings in the situation mattered little to me, he had frightened me enough that crossing him seemed unwise, and I wasn't entirely sure how far I could push him. Even so, as I began to shiver in the cooling night air, and his breath remained that of a man who hadn't yet been claimed by sleep, I pulled his blanket across myself.

He still didn't stir, and I wondered if he was staring at the opposite wall, his eyes open, thinking about what he'd done. Was he feeling guilty for ordering abuse to the woman he'd thought he could love? Or was he simply hoping I'd fall asleep without speaking to him again?

We lay like that for what seemed like an hour. Finally, just as I'd despaired of him ever leaving me to my thoughts, even in sleep, soft snores filled the bridal chamber. I stared at the moonbeam that glinted on the far wall, and a smile spread across my face. He would never believe it was a real one, and he would never believe me if I told him the reason for it, but I knew, and that was all that mattered.

I was alive.

The king was displeased.

And Meirdre was safe.

ACKNOWLEDGMENTS

Thanks to Meghan, Cathy, and Ed.

ABOUT THE AUTHOR

Anne Wheeler grew up with her nose in a book but earned two degrees in aviation before it occurred to her she was allowed to write her own. When not working, moving, or writing her next novel, she can be found planning her next escape to the desert—camera gear included. She currently lives in Georgia with her husband, son, and herd of cats.

ALSO BY ANNE WHEELER

'Leaving Humanity'

'Last Mission'

Shadows of War

Asrian Skies

Unbroken Fire

Shattered Honor

Faded Embers

Made in the USA
Columbia, SC
09 June 2020